The Dragons of Silent Mountain

Published by Blue Dragon Publishing, LLC
Williamsburg, VA
www.BlueDragonPublishing.com
Copyright © 2021 by Dawn Brotherton

ISBN 978-1-939696-71-7 (paperback)
ISBN 978-1-939696-72-4 (ePub)

Library of Congress Control Number: 2021949842

Cover by Hakm Bin Ahmad

Printed in the U.S.A

25 24 23 22 21   1 2 3 4 5 6 7

Silent Mountain poem by Paige Ashley Brotherton

The Dragons of Silent Mountain

Dawn Brotherton

Dawn Brotherton
Feb 2022

Blue Dragon Publishing

Chapter 1

Off where the cobblestones were uneven and residents forewent the chandelier for the lone candle, a young woman walked along the lane of crowded stores and eager shoppers. Near the end of the row, where even the candles were few and far between, the shingle swayed in the breeze. The creaking of the chain was music to her ears, calling her toward her favorite spot in the city.

"Ashton!" Galileo cried from the back of the store. "You're just in time. Come, I have something to show you."

Already smiling, Ashton closed the door gently behind her. Behind the cluttered counter, Galileo's messy shock of white hair was barely visible over a clay sculpture of a slumbering dragon. Little dragon eyes twinkled at her as she crossed the room. The red tint of the hide made it appear as though the dragon rose from the earth itself.

"It's beautiful." Ashton marveled at the graceful curves of the scales that somehow made her feel as sleepy as the creature appeared to be. There was something different about this dragon, though, something she couldn't quite name.

"You haven't seen what he can do yet," her grandfather said, turning to fetch something from the shelf behind him.

Ashton, standing a head taller than the old man, watched his jaunty movements with pride. *I wish I had half his creativity.*

He returned with a small pot of oil, which he poured into a hole at the top of the slope on the sleeping dragon's back. With a well-practiced hand, Galileo used a waxed wick to capture the flame from a nearby candle and touch it ever so lightly to the nostril of the sculpture.

Almost immediately, flames leaped from the dragon, making Ashton step away in surprise. From a slightly safer distance, she admired the true beauty of what her grandfather had created. The flames, no doubt fueled by a river of oil inside the dragon's body, escaped through little slots cut in the top of the dragon so they formed the spikes running down its spine. That's what had been missing from the original sculpture, Ashton realized. But they weren't missing at all; they were simply made of fire instead of clay.

"Magnificent," Ashton said truthfully, watching her grandfather's eyes light up. Though he had undoubtedly watched the fire come to life on the dragon countless times already, his delight hadn't lessened. He crouched down again so his eyes were level with the counter, perhaps getting a different perspective on his art.

"I know," he said happily. "The Lord of Bethia has already ordered three for his home to be sent by cart within the month."

"You truly are something else," Ashton said with a laugh. "I don't think there's a baron within fifty leagues who doesn't have one of your creations adorning his home."

"Gives boring structures character," Galileo insisted, pulling a smaller dragon on a hanging lantern from underneath the counter. He walked to the front of the shop and hung it next to the door, where it was sure to attract the attention of his dedicated customers. The elderly craftsman returned to his stool and absentmindedly stroked the wings of his favorite figurine, a gleaming black dragon with sweeping horns and a proud stature. His expression was unusually content as he gazed at his sculpture, and Ashton thought she knew why.

"A new record?" she asked.

Galileo smiled slyly. "Fifteen hundred brakons."

"I understand why you won't sell that particular figure, but why won't you at least duplicate it?" Ashton asked, not for the first time.

Her grandfather was a skilled artist and could easily replicate the intricate glasswork involved, especially now that he had the stable furnace her father had helped him engineer.

But Galileo shook his head. "Brindisi must be one of a kind. She can't be copied and especially not for wealth. She'd never glow again."

"I've never seen her glow at all," Ashton said.

"Maybe you've yet to need the light," Galileo responded with a small smile.

Ashton smiled too, even though she had no idea what her grandfather meant. He often spoke in riddles she didn't understand. Galileo was the city of Olmerta's oldest active member, adored for his wise counsel, sharp wit, and of course, his fantastic dragons. He'd seen more years than Ashton could imagine, and this became obvious when his quips and comments made no sense to his seventeen-year-old granddaughter. Even when the villagers didn't understand all the old man's beliefs and habits, they valued his trade above all else.

Galileo didn't only make ornaments with wings; he loved any challenge. The sleeping dragon with flaming spikes was just the beginning. He made tools, keys, and special inventions, each with a signature dragon engraved or as an embellishment. At this point, there wasn't a house in the village that didn't have at least a dragon hairclip about.

Ashton brushed her finger across the jagged peak of a sculpted mountain, a dragon's tail winding around its base. "Grandfather, do you really think dragons live in Silent Mountain?"

"My dear, I have nothing if not faith."

"In something that you've never seen?"

"Especially in the things I've never seen."

"But why haven't we seen them?"

"Perhaps there is no need. Not yet, at least. The day will come when the skies will be filled once again with dragons."

"But is that a good thing? Most people fear the return of the dragons." Ashton looked at the floor, embarrassed to admit she doubted some of what her grandfather said.

"That's because they're listening to the wrong tales. They don't know the truth," her grandfather said.

"The stories you tell are so different from the ones coming from the palace. You tell of heroic deeds and friendship. The other stories are dark and sinister. How do you know yours are right and the others are wrong?"

Galileo gave his granddaughter a loving look. "Because your grandmother told me."

She shifted uncomfortably, tucking her short, black hair behind an ear. She loved both her grandparents, but before her grandmother disappeared, she had spouted things that didn't make any sense. Ashton had assumed the old lady's mind was going.

"Did it ever occur to you who benefits from townsfolk fearing dragons?" he asked.

She shrugged. "I can't see how it benefits anyone one way or the other."

The bell above the door jingled, and Galileo pushed himself from his stool to greet the visitor. "I'll let you think on that a while."

Ashton stroked the smooth scales down Brindisi's spine once before leaving the store.

Chapter 2

"Some might question whether his interest isn't more of an obsession," Nikolai Cabot said, his lip curling into a sneer. "He litters this town with every dragon depiction his wild imagination can conjure."

"They are a symbol of Olmerta. What harm does it do?" Lukas asked his uncle. He tore off a hunk of bread and passed it to his father sitting at his left.

"The only symbol of this city is my sigil!"

"Come, brother. A sword in a fist is too much. It screams of power, yes, but it doesn't endear those who can't afford their own sword," Earl Stephan said.

"It reminds them more of tyranny than—"

"You had no trouble picking up the sword," Nikolai cut off his nephew.

Lukas recognized the dark look in his uncle's eye and realized his misstep. Bowing his head, he saluted with his open hand over his heart. Lukas prayed for the right words to ease the tension. "Chancellor, I am your humble servant and will carry my sword where you tell me to go."

"That's what I thought." Nikolai pushed away from the dining table and stood. With his hands clasped behind his back, he paced the length of the room.

While his uncle's attention was elsewhere, Lukas placed another helping of meat on his plate; his father followed suit.

"What's going on with the town of Melak?" the chancellor asked.

"We received a fine shipment of ore from them this week. We've loaded the wagons with the lumber we promised them in payment, and they are scheduled to depart tomorrow," Stephan said between mouthfuls.

The chancellor continued his pacing, muttering to himself. "If the wagons come under attack, they may never reach Melak."

"But there's no reason to suspect an attack," Lukas said. "I'm escorting the wagon to the town. We haven't had trouble in this area for years."

Nikolai turned on Lukas. "Yes, but if something were to happen to the laden wagons, we must do everything reasonable to ensure the safety of the travelers. Don't worry about the lumber. Our debt is paid once we cross into their territory."

Lukas stopped cleaning his plate with his bread and looked at his father. Likewise, the earl was frozen midchew.

"How many men ride with you tomorrow?" Nikolai fixed Lukas with a stare.

He swallowed hard, sitting up straighter. "Ten men, Uncle."

"You've been training the young nobles, have you not? Perhaps this is an easy mission to cut their teeth on."

"Yes, sir."

"Go now, both of you. I have things to consider."

Father and son rose from the table, bowed slightly, and saluted. As they left the hall, they heard Nikolai bellow to his servants to fetch Bayard.

Outside, Lukas and his father headed for home. "What was he going on about?" Lukas asked once they had gotten far enough away from the castle to lift the feeling of watchful eyes and listening ears.

Stephan avoided looking directly at his son. "Keep your mind on your business. Do as you're told."

"But a trip to Melak is a monthly routine. We've never had trouble in the past. Why would Uncle Nikolai be speculating about bandits?"

"He probably doesn't want you getting overconfident and sloppy. Anything can happen on that journey." Stephan kicked a stone as they walked. He passed it to Lukas as he had done when his sons were little and learning to play crocus.

Lukas kicked it to his father absentmindedly. "We have drills on how to react to attacks. Do you think we should drill again tonight before setting out?"

"No, you're ready. Best wear your mail, though. Have your team dress in their full gear as well. It'll make a good impression on the people of Melak when they see you gleaming on the horizon."

They passed the rock back and forth until a bad kick sent it skittering off the footpath.

"What does Uncle Nikolai have against Galileo?" Lukas asked.

His father sighed. "It's not Galileo exactly. It's what he stands for."

"He's simply an old man who tells great stories."

"Ah, yes, but he tells stories about the days when there were dragons."

Lukas looked sideways to see if his father was serious. "Do you believe dragons are real?"

"What I believe isn't important. My brother doesn't want any talk of dragons. He perceives the stories undermine his rule."

"It's not as if believing in some oversized lizard will make a difference in whether or not people pay their tithes."

"You needn't concern yourself with Nikolai's beliefs. Just do your job."

The hardness in his tone stung Lukas. In times past, Stephan would have joined in the gentle needling of the chancellor, and they would laugh together.

By now, they had reached the gate to their sizeable manor house. Almost like a peace offering, Stephan placed a hand on his son's shoulder. "Are you still making a trip into town?"

Lukas nodded.

"Meeting up with anyone in particular?" Lukas caught the sly smile his father tried to hide.

He blushed. "I'm not a schoolboy to be mocked about a perceived infatuation, Father. I have many friends in town."

"Well, don't be late for supper. Your mother will have my head."

He watched his father push through the iron rods woven together to mark the entry into his family's estates. As the gate clanged closed, the flat surface in the center was conspicuous by its lack of a crest.

A sadness rushed over Lukas at the not-so-subtle show of power his uncle's reign had over the family.

Chapter 3

"You should see the latest dragon Grandfather has made," Ashton said as she walked with Lukas beside the lake. "Fire comes from spikes on its back."

"He has the greatest imagination. I still have the dragon he carved for me when we were little. Remember? The ones we painted? Mine was fiery red," Lukas said.

"I still have my blue one by my bedside."

They walked in comfortable silence for a time.

"Did your uncle say any more about your match?" she asked, trying to keep her voice neutral.

Lukas shook his head. "No, he has other things on his mind."

"But will you at least get to meet her first?"

He shot her a look that warned her to stop nagging him.

She changed the subject. "What do you have planned for tomorrow?"

He stooped to pick up a rock and skipped it across the pond. "I'm escorting a wagon of lumber to Melak."

She rolled her eyes. "That sounds exciting."

"Mayhaps." He had gone unusually quiet.

"Shall I ride along? I haven't been to the boundary in ages. My Sheba would enjoy the change in scenery as much as I would."

"No, next time maybe. Listen, I should be going. It'll be a long ride tomorrow, and I need to ensure the wagons are secure and the team ready."

"Okay." Ashton was surprised and more than a little disappointed. "Come find me when you return, and we can practice our archery. I've gotten quite good. I think I'll earn back that five brakons I lost last time."

"Sure," he replied absently, then he returned the way they had come without so much as a wave.

Ashton picked up a flat stone, tracing the edges with her finger before sending it skipping across the mirror surface of the water that reflected the dark clouds above the Silent Mountain. "One, two, three, four, five!" And Lukas wasn't here to see it.

Ashton heard the rumble before she felt it. A tremor shook the ground, causing the water to lap against the boulders as if trying to escape. There it was, again. If not for the damp rocks, she would have thought she imagined it.

She wondered if her grandfather felt it, too.

Where the lake met the main road to town, Ashton followed the mule carts and villagers who were hauling their fresh catch to the market. Lost in her thoughts, she idly tossed a chip of bluestone into the air and caught it.

A firebolt broke across the darkening sky.

Villagers stopped, gazing in wonder at the display. Moments later, another stream of fire caught the thatched roof of the tailor shop, and it went up in a *whoosh*. Screams came from within. Villagers scattered; some toward the safety of the trees, others to fetch buckets of water.

15

At first, Ashton couldn't believe her eyes. *Fire in the sky?* It made no sense. She had never seen lightning like this.

A hand grabbed her sleeve and pulled her along. Shaking her head to regain her focus, she followed the stranger and fell in position beside fellow villagers for the bucket brigade.

A strong wind blew across her face, and Ashton looked to see if the fire would spread. The flames still shot directly skyward. She stole a glance at the trees, but their leaves weren't even stirring. She received the water bucket handed to her, quickly turned, and passed it down the line, turning to get the next one. Even amidst the shouts of terror and commands to assist with the fire, she marked the breeze as significant in this otherwise calm weather.

It seemed like hours before the blaze was extinguished. The wounded were stretched out on the grass in the center of the town square. Ashton watched as the healer covered the face of one with a grimy sheet. As the bucket brigade broke up, she worked out the kinks in her back and legs. Her arms were leaden weights from passing the heavy load for so long without a break.

Stumbling, she traced the path the buckets had followed. Others were already immersed in the icy waters of the Moss River, still fully clothed. Ashton joined them and dunked her head to rinse the soot from her hair, thankful it was short and easy to deal with. Her mother had braided her long hair, but after she died, a little girl's hair was too much for her grandfather to handle.

Washing quickly, she spent as little time in the chilly water as necessary. Tomorrow she would take a proper bath in the Silent River, where the waters ran warm. For now, she was grateful to have the acrid smell of smoke and burnt flesh mostly washed away.

She made her way home along the river rather than using the lane to town. When she found the right path, Ashton followed it into the dark forest, the cricket chirps and frog croaks accompanying her. Even without the moonlight, her footsteps were sure and confident. Nearby, she sensed something larger tracking her passing. She had lived long enough to know there were many creatures in the world; as long as she didn't bother them, they didn't bother her.

By the time she broke free from the trees and reached her front door, she was shivering from the cool air on her soaked clothes. She stripped down as much as she dared, leaving her wet things outside, then dashed into the cottage for a warm blanket.

Her grandfather sat by the hearth working a piece of wood with his knife. Having changed into dry britches and a tunic, Ashton joined him at the fire. She allowed the warmth to seep into her as she watched her grandfather work.

"Thanks for starting the fire," she finally said.

"You looked like a drowned rat," Galileo said. "What happened?"

"Didn't you hear? The tailor shop caught fire."

Galileo dropped his hands to his lap. "Was Clivus mixing his dyes again?"

Ashton shook her head. "I know this sounds silly, but I swear the fire came from the sky."

"There were no storms today, girl. Only a few dark clouds over the lake."

"I didn't say it was a storm."

The glow of the fire cast shadows from the goosebumps on Galileo's arms.

He peered at her under his bushy eyebrows. "Are you sure? Tell me exactly what you saw."

She cleared her throat, feeling a little foolish. "From nowhere, a flame streaked across the sky. I thought for sure it was my imagination. A few seconds later, another shot struck the roof of the tailor shop. After that, everything was in chaos. People running and screaming." Ashton's voice trailed off.

"There's something you aren't telling me."

"You'll think I'm crazy."

He placed a rough hand on her shoulder. "I'm the crazy one in this family. There's no room for another."

She offered a small smile and took a deep breath. "For a second—but only a second—I thought I saw something else in the sky."

"Did this something have wings?"

She stared at him. "But how did—"

He waved away her question. "It was in the sky. How else would it get there?"

She chuckled at his calm acceptance, then she became serious again. "There was a flash of color when the flames were . . . released. Then it was gone."

"Did anyone else see this?"

She shook her head. "Not that I know of. No one said anything, and I wasn't about to blurt it out. We were a little busy dealing with the fire."

"Others didn't see. I wonder why." He stroked the wood he was holding with his thumb, speaking more to himself than Ashton.

"Grandfather, you can't be thinking of dragons. I know the stories, but there has to be another explanation."

Suddenly, he jumped to his feet. "I need to go to the shop. Don't leave without putting that fire out. One disaster today is more than we need."

"But, Grandfather, what's—"

"Don't you worry about it. We'll talk when I return." With that, he was out the door.

Ashton picked up the piece of wood her grandfather had been working on. She could barely make out the head of the dragon trying to break free from the block.

Chapter 4

It was well past midnight when her grandfather returned. Ashton padded out of her room wearing a long nightdress, her feet bare. The lantern she carried cast shadows around the room.

"What's going on?"

Galileo was distracted. Ashton guided him to a chair at the table, covering his lap with a quilt made by her grandmother.

"Have you eaten anything? You ran out of here so fast, you missed dinner." She hurried to put together a cold meal of meat pie and fruit. "I can warm some stew for you if you like."

He said nothing, lost in thought. When Ashton placed his dinner in front of him, he pushed the food around with his knife, not even pretending to eat.

"I know it's not like Mama used to make, but my cooking isn't that bad." Just mentioning her mother caused a lump in her throat.

Looking up, he attempted a smile for her sake. "I'm sure it's wonderful. I'm not hungry, that's all."

"What has you so anxious?"

"They're back," he said in a hushed voice.

"Who's back?"

"The dragons."

"What? That doesn't make sense. Dragons are . . ."

"Not real? Is that what you were going to say? After all I've taught you? Don't you listen to my words?" The disappointment showed on his face and shot an arrow through Ashton.

"I . . . I don't understand," she stammered. "Assuming dragons are real, why would one attack our village? You said they were our friends."

"They were." He ran a gnarled hand through his thinning white hair, leaving it sticking out at odd angles. "Something's wrong."

She collapsed into the chair across from him. She had never seen her grandfather this way. "How long has it been since they were seen in the sky?"

Galileo stood, stepping on the quilt now puddled on the floor at his feet. He picked his carving knife and block of wood from the mantle. Inspecting the grain, he turned the emerging dragon one way then the other, catching the lantern light. "I've told you stories of the dragons in the early days when they lived in harmony with humans."

"I remember. The woman found a dragon egg and kept it safe until it hatched. The baby returned to its family of dragons. When it was fully grown, it came to the old woman to express its thanks. Thus began the partnership between human and dragon."

"I've spared you the details of when humans fell from grace, causing a rift between our kinds." His knife worked as he spoke. "Those stories have fallen away over the years. No one wants to talk of the evil things we've done. People would rather pretend they didn't happen and not take the responsibility."

Ashton wrapped the discarded blanket around her shoulders as Galileo took up his tale.

"Men grew foolish and arrogant. They didn't understand the many blessings it was to have dragons on their side. They resented raising livestock to keep the dragons fed and set out to cull their numbers through hunting, even going so far as to make a sport of it." He shuddered.

"Villager turned against villager. We are descendants of those who were against this behavior. Your grandmother's ancestors led the people who fought to save the dragons. They destroyed the traps, and the dragons disappeared."

"Where did they go?" Ashton asked.

Galileo only shrugged. "At one time, some knew the secret. But the affairs of man got in the way."

Ashton positioned herself directly in front of her grandfather, forcing him to look up from his whittling. "But why have they returned now? Can we stop them?"

Moisture stood in his eyes as he took her in. "Only the queen dragon can stop them."

For years she had heard the stories but thought that's all they were—stories. She prayed her grandfather wasn't losing it.

"So how do we find her?" she asked when he seemed to drift into his thoughts again.

"That's why I went to the shop tonight. There must be some way to find them again—to make peace." Returning the carving to the mantle, he wiped his hands on his worn trousers. "I've been saving this book to pass on to you when you were older. I don't know how accurate it is or even what it holds." He pulled out a blue leather-bound book, tattered at the corners. His fingers traced the strange symbol embossed into the hide.

"Before she left us . . . unexpectedly, your grandmother passed this to your mother." Galileo swallowed his emotions. He didn't often mention her grandmother's disappearance. "When your mother died, I saved it for you."

He took Ashton's hand and turned it palm up. Gently, he placed the small book in her grasp.

She was surprised at the weight. She started to open the cover, but Galileo stopped her.

"This is for no one else's eyes."

"Why me?"

"Read it, and maybe it will explain." He patted her hand covering the book. "I'm going to turn in. We'll talk more tomorrow."

The old man turned from the room; his usual spry step replaced with a weary shuffle.

Ashton took the seat by the empty hearth. Her mother had once held this same book. Perhaps she also sat by the light of the fire when her mother gave it to her. She wished her mother was with her now so they could read together as they used to. Her parents died more than fifteen years ago, but the memory was still painful. When they left on their trip, they promised to bring back a surprise. A twinge of guilt and shame caused her heart to pound when she remembered how angry she was when her grandfather said her parents weren't coming back. As a young child, her first thought had been that she wasn't going to get her gift.

Taking a deep breath, she said a silent prayer for her parents and her grandparents. Then she opened the cover.

Chapter 5

The horse danced nervously as Lukas waited for the final check on the convoy to be completed. He patted Zephyr's flank, knowing she was picking up on his unease. He took a deep breath, trying to calm his thoughts.

"Sir, we're ready to head out." The soldier saluted Lukas and waited at attention for acknowledgment.

Lukas looked over the snaking line of horses, soldiers, and wagons. He nodded. "Let's move."

A bugle sounded, and the lead horses stepped off, the rest of the line inch-worming behind them. While he waited to take his place, the young nobleman thought again about his uncle and his strange behavior. Not for the first time, he thought about his service to the village chancellor and what he would be doing if it were left up to him.

He pictured a small farm and a schoolroom where he could instruct his own children alongside any others in the village who were eager to learn. Master Gena, who had taught him and Ashton, would laugh at his desire to become a scholar. He didn't show much interest in schooling back then, but he appreciated all the opportunities it opened. At least for others.

He sighed.

As it was, he couldn't even marry who he wanted to.

Clucking his tongue at Zephyr, Lukas joined the column midway through the quarter-mile-long caravan. He brushed aside his self-doubt. He knew better than most that Chancellor Cabot would get what he wanted one way or the other. It was easier to stay on his good side and be in the know.

The second sun was high overhead when the bugle sound announced a halt for nourishment. Time had passed quickly; they had already entered Melak territory. Gladly, Lukas lowered himself out of the saddle and stretched his legs. The extra weight from his chain mail made his shoulders and back ache more than usual. He made circular motions with his arms to loosen his shoulders.

Around him, riders dismounted, strapping feedbags onto their horses while young boys and girls delivered pails of water up and down the line. He ruffled the hair of one towhead as she ran by, sloshing water over her clothes. It wasn't so long ago when he and Ashton were delivering water for the horses during caravans.

"You didn't spill quite that much water, but it was close."

Surprised, Lukas turned to see Ashton at his elbow. "I was just thinking of you, and you appear. That's a little bizarre," he said.

"At least you weren't up to no good when you summoned me from thin air." Ashton elbowed him playfully in the ribs, then rubbed her arm where she had struck the mail. "What's up with the extra metal?"

His delight at seeing her turned to dismay. "I'm on official business. What are you doing here? I told you this wasn't a trip for you."

"Actually, you said it would be a long ride. I gave you a head start, then allowed my mare a good run to catch up with you. With a group moving this slowly, it wasn't much of a challenge. Besides, I have to tell you what I saw last night."

A young lad handed Lukas and Ashton each a package wrapped in brown cloth. Indicating for Ashton to join him, Lukas plopped down under a nearby tree. She settled with her back against the bark, opening her meal. She peeked at the contents between the bread and held the sandwich out to Lukas. Lukas handed his sandwich over without bothering to check.

He took a large bite, closing his eyes in gratitude.

"So, what did you see?" he asked once he had swallowed.

"Did you hear about the fire last night?" Ashton wiped her mouth with the back of her hand.

"Of course. You rode all the way here to tell me about that?"

"No. I saw what might have *caused* the fire," she said.

"I heard the tailor was experimenting with colors again and something went wrong." Lukas passed her a waterskin.

She took a drink, then turned to face him. "I think it came from the sky."

"What came from the sky?"

"The source of the fire. Whatever caused the shop to go up in flames," Ashton insisted.

Lukas gave her a wary look. "You probably saw sparks floating above the fire."

Shaking her head vigorously, she dismissed his words. "No way. What I saw was before the fire. Or it was the fire. I'm not sure."

"What are you talking about? Sounds like the ride out here took more out of you than it should have."

Ashton looked around to make sure no one was paying them any attention. "Do you believe in dragons?"

Lukas laughed and water dribbled down his chin. "Look what you made me do."

"Worried you might rust? Don't avoid the question."

"Dragons? My father and I were talking about the very subject last night." He didn't mention that Uncle Nikolai and Stephan thought Galileo was a bit off.

Suddenly a bugle sounded over the chatter of the soldiers and merchants of the caravan. Lukas jumped to his feet, drawing his sword.

"What is it? What's happening?" Ashton stood beside him.

He glanced at her. "Get the extra sword from Zephyr's pack."

"What? Why?"

"Do as I say!"

Ashton ran to the horse and worked the buckle to release the sword. The shouts from the guards trying to get control of the situation added to the confusion.

A young page ran to Lukas. "Sir, bandits have overtaken the tail of the caravan."

"What of the rear guards?"

"No sign." A spray of blood shot from the page's lips. Lukas caught the boy as the lad fell into his arms, an arrow shaft protruding from the center of his back.

"Do I have your attention, Lukas of Olmerta?" came a voice above the din.

Lukas laid the boy aside as humanely and as quickly as possible, freeing his sword hand.

"What kind of coward shoots an unarmed boy in the back?"

"The kind who would rather spill as little blood as possible. Consider this the token sacrifice," a voice from the trees said.

Lukas scanned the trees but couldn't pick out a target.

"Have your soldiers step away from the wagons, and we'll be on our way. No one else need be hurt." From his left, Lukas heard steel on steel as his soldiers engaged the attackers at the front of the line. A young boy screamed. Then only sobs from the merchants in the front wagons could be heard.

"We only want the contents of your wagons. You can return to Olmerta and live to fight another day." The voice seemed to be coming from a different direction now.

Lukas scanned the line. He was responsible for at least fifty lives, fewer now, with the dead page at his feet. There hadn't been bandits along this trail in so many years, no one could recall the last encounter. Why now? Had things gotten so bad in the outer cities that ruffians were overflowing to the borders?

"I want no more bloodshed," Lukas said aloud while thinking, *except yours.* "Call your men off." His father often said things can be replaced; people could not.

A whistle sounded, followed by a chuckle from the voice. "Now that wasn't so h—"

Lukas caught the glint of metal, then the voice was cut off. A thump of something heavy falling was eerie in the silence that followed.

"Attack!" Lukas shouted.

Instantly, the sound of swords clashing and savage yells filled the forest. The bandits who had presumed victory were caught off guard as the remaining soldiers seized the advantage. Lukas entered the fray, placing himself between the thieves and the wagons. He quickly cut down four of the intruders, then turned to assist his soldiers toward the rear of the caravan.

As he ran his sword through a fifth man, Lukas noticed the lack of battle noises.

"Sound off," he called.

"Lead clear, one down."

"Mid-front clear, all accounted for."

"Middle clear, all accounted for."

"Mid-rear clear, two down."

Lukas waited, but no calls from the rear guard came.

Without bothering to mount Zephyr, he ran to the end of the line; the carnage was severe.

"Rear clear, all down." Ashton's voice was raspy through her labored breathing. She wiped her blade on the bandit at her feet. Blood dappled her face like red freckles. In a wagon nearby, a driver huddled over his wife and child, trying to shield them against the onslaught.

Lukas, fearful of startling Ashton, approached with care.

"Are you injured?"

She glanced at her arms and legs, taking stock of her condition.

"No. I'm in one piece. You?"

He shook his head. Glancing around, he caught sight of a lone merchant driver standing in his cart. "Account for your people. Report any injuries."

The man stared at him.

"Now! Go!"

Trembling, the driver climbed from the wagon and started his account, going from wagon to wagon up the line.

Ashton held out the sword to Lukas. "Thanks for letting me borrow this."

"Keep it. And I'm sure I owe you more than five brakons for taking out the leader."

She shrugged. "I was tired of his bluster."

Chapter 6

"How did this happen?" Chancellor Nikolai's voice remained disconcertingly calm.

Lukas stood at attention in front of his uncle in the throne room. "We stopped for a midday meal. My soldiers in the rearguard were overtaken before anyone spotted the bandits."

"Then how is it your remaining guards were able to overpower such a large number of aggressors? You started with only ten."

"After our discussion, you got me thinking about the possibilities of an attack, and I realized ten wasn't enough. I doubled my numbers and armed some of the merchants. When the leader was cut down—" Lukas stopped himself before he mentioned Ashton's name. "The thieves were caught off guard. We turned the tables and were able to subdue them."

"Did any survive to talk?" Nikolai's knuckles were white from his grip on the wooden arms of the throne.

"Unfortunately, no, Uncle. Eleven were killed. More probably ran away. But no townspeople from Melak were seriously injured. I lost seven soldiers and my page. We were able to deliver the lumber to Melak as promised and returned with no further incident. We plan on honoring our dead tomorrow as the second sun sets."

He watched as the chancellor fumed. Lukas couldn't tell what upset him more—the loss of his soldiers or Lukas's inability to capture a rebel.

"We inspected the enemy's dead bodies. They carried no identifying markings or crests. We brought the weapons but left the bodies where they fell for the animals to take care of." Lukas suppressed a shudder at the memory of the half-eaten corpses they encountered on their return trip from Melak.

Nikolai waved his hand in dismissal. Lukas gave a curt bow and retreated from the throne room.

Outside, he took in a deep breath, willing himself to relax. He wiped the sweat from his brow, then loosened the collar on his fresh uniform.

"Well, what did he say?" Ashton was at his side without warning, causing him to jump.

"How do you keep doing that?"

"Doing what?"

"Sneaking up on me," Lukas said.

"I wasn't sneaking. You weren't paying attention. Now tell me, what did he say? Are you in trouble?"

He shook his head. "He was irritated, for sure, but he didn't rail on me. Perhaps he was pleased I had taken his warning and doubled my guard."

"Or perhaps he's relieved he has eight fewer people to pay," Ashton said.

Lukas looked over his shoulder, then at Ashton. "You shouldn't talk that way. Nikolai isn't as bad as all that."

"From what I hear, he's much worse. Even the stories you tell don't paint him in a rosy light."

"You don't know the burden he carries every day. Ruling must be hard with many troubles we could never imagine."

"I will allow your excuses because he's your family."

They walked in silence for a time.

"You didn't tell him I was there, did you?" Ashton finally asked.

A wave of guilt rushed over him. "No. I didn't think it would help the situation."

"I agree with you."

Lukas looked at her, surprised. "Really? I thought you'd be angry."

"Nah, I don't need songs of bravery sung about me. If that happened, my grandfather might find out."

He flinched. "I didn't even consider Galileo. How did you get past him? You were a bit of a mess."

"While you went on to Melak, I stopped by the Silent River on the way home. I took a long soak in the warm water while scrubbing out my clothes. Grandfather wasn't even home when I returned. He was in the shop with his dragons."

"Dragons. Weren't you saying something about dragons before the fighting began?" Lukas asked.

Ashton at once became excited. "Oh, yes! It feels like so long ago now." She took a deep breath, then exhaled with exaggerated slowness. "I. Saw. A. Dragon."

"What?" Lukas must have heard wrong.

"I saw a dragon. Or at least part of one. I think."

"Are you sure you didn't get hit during the fighting? There are no such things as dragons," Lukas said.

"I saw it *before* the fight. And Grandfather says dragons do exist."

He wasn't sure what to say to his oldest and dearest friend. He wanted to support her, but he didn't want people to believe she was as crazy as Galileo.

"If you saw a dragon—and that's a big *if*—why now? Where have they been?" he asked.

"I'm not sure. It must be why Galileo locked himself in his shop. He's looking for clues in the old records left behind by our ancestors." She pulled out the tattered leather book. "He saved this one for me. It was my grandmother's, given to her by her mother. It talks about the dragons. Real ones! When they were everywhere."

Lukas reached out to take the book, but Ashton pulled it away.

"I'm not supposed to show it to anyone. Grandfather said it's for my daughters."

Lukas laughed. "I can't picture you braiding hair and sewing smocks."

"Perhaps my husband will be in charge of the sewing. And I can braid, thank you."

"Are you allowed to tell me what the book says, at least?"

"I suppose so." They arrived at the river and settled into their favorite spot under the willow tree. Lukas removed his jacket, tossing it over a branch. He laid down in the grass with his hands clasped over his stomach, taking in a deep breath of the rich dirt that always reminded him of playing forts with Roland when they were young. Ashton settled beside him, sitting with her legs crossed, the book opened in her lap.

"Dragons are very loyal creatures, and they're also very discerning. They don't show themselves to just anyone. You have to earn their loyalty."

"And how does one earn the loyalty of a dragon?"

Lukas saw Ashton's face turn to stone; his mocking tone was not appreciated.

"I'm sorry. After all the years of hearing Galileo tell dragon stories, I never put much credence in them. I thought they were to entertain us." He sat up and looked her directly in the eyes. "Tell me true, did you believe in dragons before a few nights ago?"

She dropped his gaze. "Sort of. I hoped they existed. I liked the idea of dragons watching over us, keeping us safe."

"Safe from what?"

Ashton plucked a blade of grass, pulling it apart from tip to root, releasing a fresh scent. "Things we cannot see perhaps. If the danger was stopped before it got to us, we might not even know it."

Lukas laid down again. "If they're protecting us, why did one catch the tailor shop on fire?"

"That's been bothering me as well. Maybe it was an accident."

"Like a misfire? It was aiming at something else and caught the roof? Doesn't sound likely."

Ashton stretched out on the grass and put her head next to Lukas's. "I think I'm the only one who saw it."

"Have you heard no other talk about it around town?"

"No. I wandered about all yesterday, listening for the juiciest gossip. I heard more about the tailor's potential escapades than any person should know, but no talk about fire in the sky. And certainly no mention of dragons."

"Maybe it's because you were looking for dragons."

She shot him a withering glance. "I *don't* go around looking for dragons in the sky."

"That's not what I meant. I mean, your mind is open to the possibility where other people aren't."

"My grandfather would have seen it." Ashton sighed. "If only he had been with me."

"It wouldn't help Galileo to be talking about dragons flying around Olmerta with Chancellor Cabot in such a mood. I can't imagine how he would react."

"What does your uncle have against Galileo anyway?"

"Funny, I asked my father that same question. He said Nikolai doesn't want people to accept Galileo's stories are true. Maybe Nikolai knows more about the dragons than he's ever said."

Ashton gave a derisive snort. "I can't imagine Nikolai believing in anything other than himself."

"So why now? If the dragons have returned, what do they want?" Lukas asked.

"Grandfather says only the queen knows."

"The queen?"

"The queen of all dragons." She opened the leather book, holding it aloft while she lay on her back reading. "She's the oldest female and hatches the largest clutches. Other dragons—both male and female—can lay eggs, but they tend to be smaller and fewer than the queen's eggs."

"Wait. If they can all lay eggs, what is the difference between a male and a female?"

"They still need both a male and a female to fertilize eggs. I'm not clear on how it's decided who carries the eggs, but only a female's eggs can reproduce. A male can lay an egg and it may hatch, but that dragon is sterile."

"It says that in your book? How did the author know?"

"People of Olmerta used to be friends with the dragons. They could communicate somehow.

Then something happened and the humans started hunting dragons. Grandfather says the men did it to cull out the numbers because dragons were getting too powerful."

"If they were so powerful, why didn't they wipe out the humans?" Lukas asked.

"The queen must have known all humans weren't the same and shouldn't be treated that way. The book says my great-great-great—I lost track of how many—grandmother helped to rescue the dragons, and they disappeared."

"Where?"

"They didn't write it down. They probably didn't want the wrong people to find out."

"I wonder if they're still there. How long do they live?" he asked.

"The only deaths of dragons the book talks about are those caused by men. Maybe that was the problem. If they never die, they would quickly outnumber humans." Ashton rested the book on her chest. "Maybe the only way to know is to find the queen."

Lukas rolled over on his side to face her. "We still don't know if you actually saw a dragon. Nothing else has happened since then. I'd rather you didn't take off on a wild goose chase. There may be things more dangerous than giant lizards."

"Like bandits? As you've seen, I can handle a sword."

Ashton pushed herself to her feet and brushed the dirt from her clothes. Offering a hand to Lukas, she said, "Time to get you back, Sir Lukas. I've kept you from your duties long enough."

He took her hand and got up. Retrieving his jacket from the tree branch, he said, "Remember, there's no need to go looking for trouble."

Chapter 7

Lukas mulled over his discussion with Ashton as he pushed through the gates to his family's property. He found his father pacing in the front hall.

"Father, what has you on edge?"

"Oh, good. You're home. Nikolai sent for us; I thought I'd have to go searching for you. At least you look presentable, although a little wrinkled." Stephan brushed a leaf from Lukas's shoulder.

"What's happened?" Lukas asked as his father ushered him toward the door.

"Who's to say with Nikolai. He may only need someone to listen to him think out loud."

"Doesn't he have Bayard for that?" Lukas was disgusted by the weaselly man who was never far from his uncle's elbow.

Stephan ignored the comment and hurried toward the palace. Lukas had to extend his stride to keep up with his father.

When they reached the throne room, Nikolai was barking out orders as minions scurried to do his bidding. Before they had a chance to render the proper courtesies, the chancellor waved Lukas and Stephan forward.

"That old man is at it again," Nikolai said without preamble. "Can't he keep his mouth shut?"

The two looked at him, perplexed.

"Galileo! That old fool! Dragons are all people are talking about. They're excited for the return of their precious pets. I need people at work. Not standing around yammering about flying lizards."

"Brother, is that why you called us here? Do you need us to pay him a visit?"

Nikolai scoffed. "As if you had the power to scare even an old man." He scribbled his signature on a scroll one of his servants put in front of him.

Lukas's face grew hot as he fought the urge to make a biting remark that wouldn't help anyone. Instead, he managed to control his tone as he said, "What can we do for you, Chancellor?"

Nikolai fixed him with a hard stare. "I have reports of deserters from the guard posts during the night."

Lukas felt the words like a blow. "No, that can't be right. There must be some other explanation."

"That's what I need you to figure out. If they are deserters, I expect you to hunt them down and give them the proper punishment."

Stephan jumped in before his son said anything in anger. "Who's missing?"

Nikolai waved his hand, and a young girl scurried to present a parchment to Stephan.

Stephan looked at the list. "There are nine names here," he said in shock.

Lukas snatched the list from his hand, running his eyes quickly over the names. He looked up at his uncle. "There's no way these soldiers left their posts voluntarily."

"Maybe it's those bandits you let escape. They're coming for revenge." Nikolai's eyes danced with something bordering on humor.

"We'll look into it," Stephan said, taking his son's elbow. Before they even reached the door, Nikolai's attention was on other things.

Lukas stomped off in a huff, and this time, his father had to hurry to catch him. When Stephan touched his sleeve, Lukas turned on him. "My people are not deserters! How dare he not show the slightest compassion for their fate!"

"We'll figure it out. Let's split the list and go visit their homes. Why don't you call up your second and get her talking to the other soldiers? See what they know."

Lukas ripped the paper and thrust half toward his father. Then he went to find Lieutenant Raquel. He wanted to know why he had to hear about this from his uncle rather than from her.

He found her in the barracks going through lockers. "You aren't going to find them in there." His voice was harsh.

Lieutenant Raquel came to attention. "Sir, I'm looking for reasons why they might have gone missing."

While only a few soldiers lived in the barracks, they each had lockers and trunks where they could store work-related items. By the disarray of the room, Raquel had almost finished her search.

"Wouldn't it have been more prudent to have looked for me instead? Before the chancellor did?" He tried to contain his anger, but it seeped through.

"Sir, I tried. I sent messengers. You weren't to be found."

Lukas dropped his eyes. He had been with Ashton at the river. No one would know to look there.

He relaxed his tone. "Stand easy. What have you discovered?"

Raquel spread her feet to shoulder-width but didn't stand much easier. "Sir, I haven't located any clues in here yet. Everything is exactly as it should be. No one saw the soldiers leave or be taken. There was no blood or signs of foul play at their posts. It's as if they simply vanished."

"We can rule out magical disappearance. What's next?"

"Now that you're here, we can talk to the families. I was waiting in case . . . she didn't finish her thought.

It was the commander's job to notify loved ones of tragedy. It was also a job Lukas was sure Raquel didn't want to experience yet. No one ever did.

"My father and I will talk to the families. Finish up here, then go to the pub and listen to the gossip. Sometimes it contains a bit of truth."

She came to attention and saluted.

Lukas returned her salute and left the barracks.

All the soldiers were housed in the same area of Olmerta near the barracks where they could respond quickly if needed. As the son of the earl, Lukas was an exception because their home was close to the palace anyway.

He straightened his jacket as he walked toward the house first on his list and prayed to whatever gods were listening that he would get through these notifications without emotion.

A shadow briefly darkened the path in front of him before clearing to the brightness of the sun. Lukas looked over his shoulder for the source but saw nothing.

Chapter 8

Ashton brushed the cobwebs aside as she reached into the dark corner of the musty basement for the trunk.

"This one?" she asked Galileo. It took all her strength to pull the large trunk into the dim candlelight.

"I think so. Oh, I wish I could remember exactly where I put those pages. Your grandmother was the one who always kept me organized. She'd be throwing a fit if she saw the shape of the shop now."

"This has a lock on it. Do you have the key?" Ashton didn't hold out much hope he could find it, even if it wasn't lost long ago.

"We don't need a key." Her grandfather moved to the opposite side of the trunk. With a few quick twists and turns of the leather straps, the lid was free, and he pried it open to reveal stacks of parchments and books. "The lock is for show."

He kneeled in front of the container that came up to his chest.

"That's going to take you forever to go through," Ashton said.

He was already absorbed in his search.

"Why don't we take this upstairs so you can work in better lighting?" she suggested. He didn't respond until she took his arm and pulled him to his feet. "Go. I'll bring you things to look through."

She loaded her arms and hurried after him as he carried the only source of light.

After getting him settled at the counter, she lit a lantern and went down for another load. When she emerged from her ninth or tenth trip—it *felt* like a hundred trips, and she'd lost count—Ashton was short of breath. The stack of papers she'd placed at her grandfather's feet, however, had grown quite tall. She'd always suspected he was a packrat; now, there was no doubt.

Engrossed in his task, Galileo added some records to a smaller pile at his elbow. Ashton assumed he found some things requiring a closer look.

On her next descent, a drawing on the top of the stack in the trunk caught the light and distracted her. As the candle flickered, the object on the page appeared to dance. Ashton pulled it closer to study it.

Before she had a chance to read the words underneath the picture, heavy footsteps overhead grabbed her attention.

Emerging from the dank basement, the crowd assembled in the tiny shop caught her off guard. She pushed her way through to find her grandfather holding court among the people at his counter.

"Some of my livestock have gone missing," one woman explained. "At first I thought they must have slipped through the fence, but then Jordi told me her flock was thinning as well."

"I've seen colors in the sky that shouldn't be there. Streaks of greens and browns," another person called out.

"Do you really think it's time? Are the dragons back?"

"Of course they're back," Ashton heard her grandfather say. "My granddaughter saw one."

The people started talking and asking questions all at once. When they spotted her, some whispered and pointed. Adults held small children up so they could see over the crowd.

"Grandfather," Ashton hissed. "What are you doing?"

"Here she is now. Come, child." Galileo reached for Ashton.

She stood beside him, looking over the gathering. Her grandfather went on. "We knew the dragons weren't gone for good. They had their reasons for leaving, and they'll reappear when they're ready."

"I saw one pick up a goat and eat it whole!" a youngster of seven said triumphantly. The group laughed, and his father patted his head.

Galileo signaled with his arms for people to quiet down. In time, only shuffling feet and an occasional cough were heard.

"I've been telling you the time would come. We only had to be patient," Galileo said. He was more animated than Ashton had ever seen him, even more than when he made a new discovery.

He put his arm around her shoulder. "You'll see. Things will be different now that the dragons have returned."

"Will there be more fires?" a voice called out.

"Why did it attack the tailor shop?" another one followed.

"A simple mistake, I'm sure," Galileo said. "I've been going through the old records. We'll need to reestablish the old feeding schedules with pens set aside for the dragons to pick from. That way, they'll leave your herds alone."

"Who's going to pay for the dragon food?" asked an older gentleman in the front.

"Isn't that why we've been paying our tithes? For protection?" someone else offered.

"According to old records, the Olmerta treasury should cover it," Galileo answered.

"Who's going to tell the chancellor?" Nervous laughter broke out across the crowd.

Galileo opened his arms wide. "I recommend you all stay vigilant. Look through any records you may have hidden in your basements or attics that may help explain what's happening. We're in this together."

People scooped items off the shelves and lined up to pay for their treasures. For the next hour, Galileo tallied the bills and made change while Ashton carefully wrapped the packages for the customers. The bell over the door jingled one last time as the final patron departed. Ashton sat down heavily on a stool. Her feet were aching.

The opposite of tired, Galileo flitted around the room, taking a dusting rag to the now almost empty shelves. "Isn't it exciting? The dragons are once again in the skies!"

Ashton hung her head. "Why did you tell everyone? We can't even be sure."

"But we are sure! We have to be."

"What brought those people here? What have you been saying? When the chancellor catches wind of it, he'll be furious!" *And Lukas won't be very happy either.*

"Ah, Nikolai wouldn't know the truth if it bit him," Galileo said. "But we know the truth. It's what your grandmother taught you long ago. Don't tell me you've forgotten?"

She looked shamefaced. She hadn't forgotten, but she also wasn't sure it explained what was happening now.

"Sing it for me."

Softly at first, but eventually giving in to the joy on his face, Ashton sang the song her grandmother taught her.

"When you feel alone, look to the east
Where sun and dragons rise
And soar over rock and leaf
Safe beneath their watchful eyes.

Together we have talked
And spent many nights in fun,
For those who fly and those who walk
Wing and arm move as one.

Our glory days show us how
We must always stand as two.
My dear, learn all you can right now
For one day, they'll look to you."

When she finished, her grandfather had tears in his eyes but a smile on his lips. "That was divine. Thank you, dear."

She absentmindedly lifted a corner of a small stack of papers and let them flip past her thumb, making rhythmic rippling noises while she thought.

"But the only sign we have of dragons is a burnt cottage. That doesn't bode well."

Galileo brushed aside her objections. "There are other signs. We merely didn't know what we were looking for until you spotted a dragon."

He rummaged through the stack of parchments on the counter. He thrust a page into her hand. The ink was clear enough to have been penned only the week before.

Two mountains towered over a huddling village below. One had snow peaks while the other top was obscured by something resembling storm clouds. Rivers flowed from each mountain, ending in a blue pool that had to be Silent Lake of their town.

"It's lovely, but I don't see your point," Ashton said.

"They've reappeared for a reason. I'm sure we'd rather have them on our side than against us, whatever is coming. Have you noticed the darkening skies around the Silent Mountain as of late?"

She thought about it, then recalled the mirror image reflected in the lake. "I do remember thinking a storm was blowing in. Did you feel the ground shake?"

He shook his head. "Something is happening on that mountain. You mark my words."

"You've always told me nothing good comes from the Silent Mountain, that creatures living there can't be killed with a crossbow. Or were those nothing but stories meant to keep Lukas and me from wandering too far?"

"The legends are true. No one who has entered the woods at the base of the mountain has returned. It has been that way for as long as anyone can remember." He shifted through the papers again and pulled out an accounting sheet of some sort.

"This is a record of journey-people who have set out to cross the mountain. They took enough supplies to last months, goods to trade, and even livestock to sacrifice if they were attacked by wild beasts. None ever came home."

"Well, maybe they found what they were looking for on the other side and decided to stay," she said.

Galileo shook his head vigorously. "We can go *around* the mountain. It takes a long time, but it's been done. No one's ever come *through* the foothills to other side of the mountain."

Chapter 9

Ashton walked by the iron gate for the third time in a very short period.

"Ashton darling, you are always welcome here. Quit lurking outside and come in," Lukas's mother called from the front door. She set a plate of biscuits on the table as Ashton entered.

"I'm sorry, Lady Melea. I didn't mean to disturb you."

"I could use a bit of company. The boys have been out all day, and I'd rather not eat alone." She poured hot liquid into a clay mug. Ashton smiled when she spied her grandfather's signature dragon on the handle.

"I was waiting for Lukas. We planned to meet up after his shift, but he's unusually late."

"I have a feeling it's going to be a long night. He and his father are visiting all the families of the missing soldiers."

"What missing soldiers?"

"Nine soldiers left their posts last night. Lukas suspects foul play, and he's talking to everyone he can think of to get to the bottom of it."

Except me, Ashton thought. She picked up a biscuit and appreciated the soft consistency of the pastry, still warm from the oven. When her nose caught the sweet aroma of honey mixed with spicy-hot cinnamon, she barely stopped herself from popping the whole thing into her mouth at once in a very undignified manner.

When they were little, she and Lukas planned missions on days when his mother was baking. They mapped out the best route into and out of the kitchen without getting caught. They even planned distractions that weren't often appreciated by his parents but worked to provide time for a few extra goodies from the tray.

Melea seemed to read her mind. "If I remember correctly, these are your favorites."

Ashton smiled brightly. "Everything you make is my favorite."

"You don't have to butter me up. You may have another. I set some aside for Lukas already."

Ashton helped herself to another biscuit. "What do they think happened?"

"Nikolai is spouting nonsense about deserters, but Lukas is having none of that. When they came home at lunch, they had already talked to most of the families. No one who knows the soldiers would even suggest they would leave their families behind."

The loud clank of metal on metal sounded from the yard.

"Perhaps they're back sooner than expected." Melea stood to get more mugs from the shelf.

Lukas came through the door, followed closely by his father.

He stopped short when he caught sight of Ashton at the table. "Oh, I'm sorry. I totally forgot about our plans. I've been tied up today."

"It's all right. Your mother was filling me in. Any luck?"

Stephan kissed his wife's cheek and took a seat. "Nothing."

Lukas sank wearily into a chair. "We talked to the families of the nine soldiers. No one was having trouble. Everything was normal. Most of them had plans for today. Not something you would see if they planned on leaving."

"Well, that supports your theory that they didn't desert," Ashton said.

He gave a derisive snort. "Great. So I'm left with my uncle's theory that the bandits we chased away have returned for revenge."

"No way! They were basic thieves," Ashton caught herself barely in time, "from what you've told me. I can't imagine they would attack a palace over a caravan. If they were that ambitious, why not start with the town?"

"It doesn't make sense to me either," Lukas agreed.

"What did Lieutenant Raquel find?" Melea asked her son.

"No one saw anything. They claim the soldiers checked in as scheduled, then missed their check-in the next cycle."

"Did they all disappear at once?" Ashton asked.

"No one knows. They may have been picked off one by one in that three hour stretch." Lukas stood and started pacing. "I don't know what I'll do if this is my fault because I didn't chase the stragglers into the woods and capture them."

"You couldn't have left the merchants alone," Melea said.

"At first light, I'll inspect their posts. I doubt there's anything to see, but I don't know what else to do."

"Do you want me to go with you?" Ashton asked.

"What could you do? This is official palace business. We all know what you and your grandfather think of the palace."

Melea sucked in a sharp breath while Ashton sat stunned at the rebuke.

Stephan cut through the tension. "We could use as many eyes on this as we can get."

Ashton rose slowly. "No, I'm sure Sir Lukas can figure this out on his own. I have other things I can be doing."

"Like hunting for dragons?" Lukas snapped.

This time, it was more like a punch than a slap.

"Dragons?" Melea asked, looking from Lukas to Ashton and back.

Stephan put his hand over hers. "Nikolai is wound up by Galileo's obsession. It put him in quite the mood before we arrived at the palace today."

Trying to control her emotions, Ashton spoke directly to Lady Melea. "Thank you for your kindness and delicious biscuits. They brought back many happy memories of times long gone now." Without addressing the men, she left the cottage.

She forced herself to walk casually when all she wanted to do was run away as fast as she could. She didn't want to be around Lukas anymore. First her grandfather was telling her story to anyone who would listen, and now Lukas was throwing it in her face.

When she reached the safety of the trees, she allowed her shoulders to slump. She took in deep breaths of the cool, fresh air, which held a hint of wet bark. Staying under the shelter of the leaves, she followed the ring around the town center to connect to the path to her cottage.

Out of the corner of her eye, she caught movement. Not something small, like a forest animal. This was much bigger, much faster, and much higher. She made her way closer to the inner ring but stayed hidden behind a large oak. Her eyes were trained on the sky, but nothing else stirred.

After several motionless minutes, she gave up.

Great, now I'm seeing things, she thought as she picked up her pace toward home.

The breeze on her back was strong enough to blow the hair into her face, then it was gone. She refused to turn around.

Chapter 10

The next morning, Ashton was up with the first sun. Her grandfather had left even earlier, but she hadn't been able to pull herself from her bed. After a quick breakfast of leftover bread and jam, she was out the door. She knew her grandfather would be anxious to start replenishing his shelves, and she had to be on hand to watch the store.

In the town center, she smiled at the hustle and bustle that always preceded market days. Shop owners swept the walks and washed windows while grocers rolled carts of fresh fruits and vegetables outside their doors.

She fell in behind a family driving their sheep down the cobblestone street.

"Daddies, look!" a little boy said, pointing over Ashton's shoulder.

The men glanced around. Then stopped. A broad smile broke across their faces, and they began waving wildly.

Ashton couldn't resist any longer. She turned to see what had the men so excited. Then she froze. The wingspan on the green dragon practically covered the entire street, and it was coming closer.

Instinctively she ducked. When she heard the boy scream, she looked up; the beast's claws wrapped around one man, carrying him away.

Ashton thought she would be sick. The boy's other father scooped up the boy to protect him. People screamed and ran, knocking over carts and displays in their rush to get away. Others stood frozen in confusion, trying to decipher the bedlam that was going on.

She needed to get to her grandfather. On shaky legs, she forced herself to keep moving.

Galileo stood under the shingle outside his shop when Ashton threw herself into his arms.

"What is it, child? What's all the yelling?"

"Grandfather." That's all she got out before the sobs came.

He rocked her side to side as she cried. When she seemed to be gaining control, he asked, "Are you hurt? What's happened?"

She pulled away so she could look him in the eye. "It was a dragon."

Galileo's eyes lit up. "A dragon? You saw another one? Oh, how I wish I had been there."

"No, you don't understand. It was horrible!"

His face dropped. "Horrible?"

Tears started to fall again, but Ashton spoke through them. "The dragon plucked a man right off the street. It carried him away."

"Away where?"

"Away! Probably to eat him! Don't you get it? Dragons aren't our friends. They may be back, but it's because they're hungry."

Galileo stumbled backward and hit the wall. His legs buckled, and he slid down to the sidewalk.

"Grandfather! Are you okay?" Ashton stooped next to him. "Wait here. I'll get you some water." She ran inside and came out with a mug of water.

She put it to his lips and forced him to drink. Most of it spilled on his tunic, turning the dust there into mud. He finally waved her away.

Ashton helped him to his feet, and they went inside. Without speaking, Galileo frantically searched the papers on his desk.

"What are you looking for?" she asked.

When he didn't answer, she took his hands in hers, making him stop.

His glassy eyes stared past her to something she couldn't see. She took the paper out of his hands and studied it. It didn't seem to be anything of significance. She replaced it on the stack.

"Maybe we should go home." Silently, she gathered his things and led him to the door.

The walk home took twice the time it should have, with Galileo shuffling his feet and Ashton constantly looking over her shoulder. In the town center, storekeepers were going about their business as if nothing had happened, although the absence of customers was evident.

Inside the cottage, Ashton settled her grandfather in his bed and covered him with his favorite quilt. He still hadn't spoken another word, and this worried her.

She was getting ready to go for the healer when a knock sounded at the door. When she opened it, a scared mob confronted her. She pushed them away from the door and followed them outside, closing the door firmly behind her.

"Where is Galileo? We need to talk to him," a woman said.

"He isn't well. He can't speak with you right now," Ashton answered.

"Was it really a dragon?" someone shouted.

"It was. I saw it," came a reply from the left.

"It tore that man from the street. He hadn't done anything to provoke an attack."

"Is this what Galileo was excited to get back? Dragons killing our people? Tell him to make them go away."

"We don't want them here."

The voices came at Ashton from all directions. She wasn't sure how to respond to anyone.

"Please, please! Calm down." She was getting irritated by their accusations. "Galileo didn't call the dragons here. He doesn't have some secret communication with them."

"But he's the one who said they would return, and here they are."

"Well, he was right. But that still doesn't mean he has anything to do with this dragon. He doesn't have all the answers. At least he's trying to figure them out. What are you doing to help?"

The crowd started shouting questions again.

"I don't have your answers either. I'm going to need you to leave. Please, my grandfather needs his rest."

While some continued with their demands, others moved off quietly. Ashton assured them the best she could that Galileo would talk to them as soon as he was feeling better.

She went inside and left the remaining few standing in the yard. With her back against the door, she took in a deep breath, trying to hold herself together.

She checked on her grandfather again. He was shivering. "I'll start the fire." Once she had it stoked up to a full roar, she filled a glass of water and put it by his bedside.

With quickness she hadn't expected, Galileo grabbed her hand. "Find Brindisi."

She looked into his watery eyes. "Brindisi's at the store, Grandfather. No one will get to her."

He squeezed harder. "Beware the Cabots. Only Brindisi."

Patting his hand, she reassured him. "I'll take care of her. Don't worry."

His arm fell to the bed and his eyes closed. She pulled the blanket up to his chin and kissed him gently on the forehead.

Glancing outside and seeing the yard empty, Ashton once again made out for the healer's hut.

After fetching the healer and sending him to their cottage, Ashton went by her grandfather's shop. She wasn't sure what it was about that black dragon that had him so obsessed, but she wanted to be able to set his mind at ease.

It felt too quiet in the store without Galileo's constant tinkering and talking to himself. Brindisi was resting on the countertop amid all the clutter Ashton had brought up from the basement. Picking it up gently, Ashton moved the figurine to an almost empty shelf on the back wall.

"There you go. You'll be more comfortable up here." She smiled as she realized she was talking to the statue much the way her grandfather would. But she also found some comfort in it. At least it broke the eerie silence.

"So, Brindisi, did you find anything interesting in this pile of papers while we were gone? Would be nice if you could have tidied them up a bit." Ashton straightened the piles to keep them from spilling over. One page caught her eye.

At first, it seemed like a normal ledger, but the amounts of cattle and sheep were extremely high. She didn't think Olmerta had that many heads in the whole town. She checked the date; it was well over two hundred years ago. She glanced through the pile, pulling out other ledger pages and stacking them together. A more recent date—but still a hundred years ago—discussed caravans loaded with various supplies and crops. Ashton was surprised what a lively trade Olmerta must have carried on with neighboring towns. Nowadays, they almost exclusively traded with Melak, and that was for very limited items.

Her eye settled on a document with a drawing of a landscape. There was no color, but the scene looked vaguely familiar. She studied it closely, but the recognition was like something stuck on the edge of her vision; it wouldn't come into focus. She started a new stack for drawings.

When she began sorting the ledger pile by date, she noticed all the ledgers with caravans had the lower righthand corner tore off. Odd. Even if they had originally been bound, it wouldn't have been by a lower corner.

She turned her attention to the remaining unsorted documents. Most of them were chicken-scratch—notes jotted as a reminder, letters to family, and attempts at poems or song lyrics.

"Listen to this one, Brindisi:

"The great sun rises on the waiting world
sprawled out below
Every drop of dew, twirling leaf, and solid rock

awaits its glow
It flaunts its brightness on the best of nature its
light can show
Most of all it falls on the single mountain
untouched by snow
And the mountain is silent

"What do you think? Was the author talking about *our* Silent Mountain? I don't remember ever seeing snow there. Even when the surrounding peaks turn white in the winter." She felt foolish when she turned to the black statue, half-expecting an answer. Clearing her throat, she went on reading aloud.

"All surrounding peaks are clothed in white,
bitterly braving the cold
But there is one lone mountain whose summit
no snowflake seems to hold
It's the fires within that keep it so warm
according to the legends of old
The tales grow taller, the culprits grow larger
every time the story is told
And the mountain is silent

"The stories come from a rising power toiling
away on the ground.
Upon bustling lives, each one like the other, the
mountain sternly looks down.
The newcomer has quaint ways, moving like
ants in its town.
They whisper and talk, anxiously waiting for the
mountain to make a sound
But the mountain is silent."

Ashton's voice trailed off as she thought about the deeper meaning of the poem. If this is about Olmerta, who would be the rising power and who are the ants?

"The people make noise, oh how they do, with their swords and obsession with things
And the mountain is used brutally by those claiming to be lords and kings
The fear it inspires, simply by its silence, and its daring to be unique
What it might change if only the stone could stand up for itself and speak
But the mountain is silent

"The men fear and feint
Prophesy and paint
Use and abuse the mountain
Fuss and cause trouble
Dart through the rubble
Tell tales of the mountain
Control and conspire
Fulfill devious desires
Captivate followers with the mountain
Shout and shriek
And endlessly speak
Of nothing but the mountain
And yet the mountain remains
Silent."

As Ashton lowered the page, a chill went through her. The heaviness of the silence surrounded her. Again, she had that sensation that something was slightly out of her reach.

Chapter 11

"What's going on?" Lukas shouted over the noise of the crowd pushing toward the palace gates. The iron bars that had been open for as long as Lukas could remember were now closed, leaving the palace inaccessible to the throng.

Lieutenant Raquel came to attention and saluted before answering. "There was a disturbance near the town center. People are talking about something in the sky. Some claim it was a dragon."

Lukas couldn't catch a break. If Galileo had his followers spun up with nonsense, he was going to have to bring him in. This couldn't go on. People were going to get hurt.

He pointed at one vocal man pushing against the gate. "Him," he told the guards. "Bring him to the practice yard." He stormed away. With all the uproar, he couldn't think straight.

Moments later, two guards appeared before Lukas. While the middle-aged man they escorted seemed less enthusiastic than when backed by his peers, he was certainly not cowering.

"Tell me what's going on, and don't give me any drivel about dragons," Lukas commanded.

The man took a moment to compose his words. "I don't know how else to explain it. One minute, Frankel was there with his boy, the next minute—" He checked his words. "*Something* carried him off."

"And no one tried to stop him?"

"Stop who? Frankel?"

"No, the man who carried him off. If you all saw it happen, why did no one come to Frankel's rescue?" Lukas was annoyed.

"It wasn't a man."

Lukas waited. "Well?"

Raising one eyebrow, the man gave him a pointed look. "It was a dragon."

"For all that is holy! Where is all this talk of dragons coming from? Did Galileo put you up to this?"

"Galileo wasn't even there. I saw the green beast swoop in from nowhere and pull poor Frankel from his family."

"Not one of my soldiers has reported this. All I heard was about a disturbance on the street. Something about an overturned cart."

"Maybe that's because you forbid them to talk of dragons," the man said.

"Be on your way," Lukas said, turning his back.

"What are you going to do about it?"

He stopped. "Do about what?"

"The dragon. Are you not listening? Is the chancellor going to pay for the missing cattle?"

Lukas trudged away. He wasn't sure where to start sorting this out. Maybe it was time to talk to Galileo. Even if he wasn't behind this, he might be able to explain why the townspeople were reacting this way. Besides, he owed Ashton an apology. He shouldn't have snapped at her.

Going through the back gate to avoid the crowd, he made his way around the town center until he reached the spoke leading to the Silent Mountain Shop. He was surprised to find the door locked in the middle of the day. He pounded on the door.

After waiting several minutes, Lukas decided to try the cottage. He backtracked to the center of the wheel and took the path he had traveled so often he could do it with his eyes closed.

As he approached the door, he met the healer departing.

"Hello, sir. Is all well?" Lukas asked.

"Galileo has taken a turn. A bit of a shock is all. He'll be fine after a rest."

"Thank you for a fine job, Master Healer." Lukas started toward the cottage.

"Galileo is sleeping," the healer said.

"I won't disturb him. I'll simply have a word with Ashton."

"She's not home."

That's not like her. "Any idea when she'll return?"

"She said she'd be gone a few days. She packed a bag and rode off. I told her I'd check in on her grandfather and make sure he ate."

"Again, my thanks."

The healer left Lukas standing in the yard trying to decide his next course of action. *What could be so important?*

He tried to think where she would go that would take her days. If she felt the need to consult a different healer, she may ride to Melak, but the village healer said all Galileo needed was rest. She would at least trust in the healer until he gave her a reason not to. Besides, Melak was only a day's ride.

He didn't have time to unwrap her mystery. He still had to figure out what had happened in town and report to his uncle.

Considering what his uncle's reaction would be, Lukas's day went from bad to worse.

Chapter 12

Ashton hefted the saddle off her mare's back and used grass to wipe the sweat from Sheba's hide. The first sun had already set, and the second wasn't far behind; she wanted to set up camp before it got too dark to see.

The foothills of the Silent Mountain were ahead. Ashton had no intention of entering after dark. She'd rather not enter them at all, but she didn't see any other way.

Grandfather told her to look for Brindisi. After reading the poem and part of the blue leathered-bound journal, something told her Brindisi was more than a statue. She could no longer doubt the reality of dragons, having seen two herself. But it didn't track with the songs and stories she had been told. Dragons were supposed to be kind and loyal creatures. Even with the new information her grandfather provided about the rift between humans and dragons, why now? Why the attack? And unprovoked? It made no sense.

If her hunch was right and the mountain had something to do with the dragons, she needed to figure out the connection before anyone else got hurt.

After hobbling Sheba near fresh grasses to nibble on, she made a small fire and settled down next to it, using her pack as a pillow. She opened the little blue book her grandfather had given her only days before. *It seems like years,* she thought. So much had happened.

As she read, it was obvious dragons and humans had lived together in peace at some point.

From one queen to another, the pact was made.

But what changed? The entries in the book jumped from working alongside the dragons to learning to live without them, with no mention of why they left or if they would return.

What was the big secret hidden in these pages— pages that read more like a history lesson with a sprinkle of scientific research instead of a book filled with secrets meant only for a chosen reader? What was too sacred to be shared with others—her grandfather included? Certainly not dragon attacks, as there wasn't even anything alluding to them.

There was a lot of talk about crops and the building of the town walls. It seemed the dragons played some part in the building of the defenses of Olmerta. Nothing specific, only references to when the dragons came and how much progress was made.

After the dragons left, harvests didn't yield the same results. Some of the farmers switched out what had been the most bountiful crops to something completely different. *Ugh, that's where those green potatoes came from,* Ashton thought.

She turned the page to a glistening picture of green woods after a heavy rain; the image so realistic, she touched the page, expecting to feel the moisture on her fingertips. If this place truly existed, she hoped to visit it one day. The book closed as she rolled over to sleep.

Getting an early start, Ashton once more checked the cinch on her saddle. She stirred the ashes from the dead fire to ensure there wasn't anything left to ignite.

Mounting Sheba, she glanced back to where her village lay far in the distance out of sight. A twinge of guilt gripped her heart when she thought of her grandfather, but she knew his dream was to live in a land of dragons. It couldn't be this way, with humans and the beasts at odds. He wanted her to find Brindisi. Real or imagined, she was going to get to the heart of the dragon story. She wasn't sure how, but the Silent Mountain felt like the right place to start.

When Ashton gave a slight nudge with her heels, her mare walked onto the tree-covered path, where they were soon swallowed by the darkness. Her heart beat rapidly. It was too dark to make out a trail, but she trusted Sheba's footing.

Sticky webs crisscrossed the path, and she held her arms to guard her face from being covered. Eventually she rode into a clearing. Dismounting to stretch her legs, Ashton took the time to clear the cobwebs from Sheba's face and chest.

"You poor girl. You didn't ask for this, did you?"

Sheba nuzzled Ashton in appreciation.

Light filtered through clouds and shone down on an area about the size of her cottage and yard. The grass reached her waist, hiding whatever may be living in it. The trees circling the grass formed a tight wall with no indication of where she should go from here.

Leading Sheba by the reins, Ashton used the sword Lukas had given her to brush away the grass ahead and scare away anything that might be awaiting them.

When her sword clinked on metal, the sound startled Ashton and she jumped. Moving more cautiously, she looked closer into the overgrowth and spied a circular rim large enough for a wagon wheel with grass growing between its spokes. She found more rusted bits of metal and rods.

"Well, Sheba, looks like we found one of the caravans that tried to get through here." Ashton shuddered, wondering what had happened to the people.

She backed away from the skeleton of the cart and looked around to take in her options. The path they'd taken through the woods was gone; the trees as close together there as where they were heading. She spun again, assuming she had missed it.

This time, she spotted a slight opening in the trees, directly in Sheba's line of sight. Seeing no other option, Ashton resumed brushing the long grass from their path with the sword. Once they reached the edge of the clearing, Ashton sized up the opening, finding it only large enough to accommodate a rider on horseback. Ashton trusted Sheba's instincts on the trail and got back in the saddle, allowing the horse to lead.

The forest didn't seem nearly as dark and gloomy as the first woods they rode through. Ashton didn't know if it was because she was adjusting to the dismal surroundings, or if the light was improving. The spiderwebs here were nonexistent, which cheered her immensely.

The sense of being tracked haunted her, keeping her on high alert as she moved deeper into the woods. Many times she caught movement in the corner of her eye but couldn't locate its source. Growls and snarls, the likes of which she'd never heard, replaced the usual chirping of insects and birdsong.

Something whizzed by her ear, and Ashton whipped her head around, trying to locate an insect large enough to create such a sound. Then another whizzed by, followed closely by two or three more projectiles. Realizing she wasn't dealing with overly large insects, she spurred Sheba into action.

Only one path split the trees, so Ashton had no other option than forward. Something small and hard slammed into her, deflecting off the quiver strapped to her back. When Sheba accelerated even more, Ashton determined she might also have been hit.

Ahead, a large fallen tree blocked the path. Taking a bet on the unknown over the predator following her, Ashton kicked Sheba into an extra burst of speed to propel them over the barrier.

As they landed, Ashton's teeth clacked together, and her heart went into her throat. Sheba kept up the pace, outdistancing whatever it was that had been behind them.

At length, Ashton slowed her to a walk, then pulled her to a stop. Gently, she climbed out of the saddle and checked Sheba for any sign of injury. A welt blossomed on her right flank, but the skin was not torn. Whatever had hit her must have been a glancing blow.

Next, she removed her quiver and inspected the large chunk taken out of the frame. She shivered when she thought of the damage the projectile would have done to her back.

Standing silently, Ashton listened to the woods. No growls or sounds of pursuit, but also no insects. Only Sheba's heavy breathing. The forest was too quiet.

Chapter 13

Lukas practiced what he would say multiple times on his way to the palace. It was getting late, and Lieutenant Raquel's investigation into the incident on the square was still ongoing; so far, it was as if the townspeople had been in two different places entirely. They had either seen the dragon with green scales and broad wings as clear as day, or they had seen nothing but a bunch of people screaming and ducking.

And to top it off, there were still no clues regarding the disappearance of the missing soldiers.

When he finally got up enough courage to enter the throne room, he found his uncle in a rare mood. The chancellor seemed to be smiling.

When Lukas thought his day couldn't get weirder, Nikolai called to him. "Come, my boy. What's the news? Have you something to report?"

Lukas was taken aback. His uncle had never spoken to him affectionately. At first, he was sure he must have heard wrong.

"Come, come." Nikolai motioned him forward.

Lukas issued the proper salute and stood at attention. His rehearsed speech left him. "Sir, I'm not sure . . . I mean, it isn't clear . . ."

"Don't be so formal. Stand easy."

He shifted his feet but couldn't find a way to relax under such odd circumstances.

"I hear we have a dragon," Nikolai said.

"Sir, that's what some people are saying, but we're getting mixed reports from witnesses."

"I heard it had a wingspan that covered the width of the avenue. Pretty impressive."

"Then you probably also heard this dragon supposedly carried off a grown man. His family is devastated."

"I would imagine so. Do what you can to ease their suffering. Are you sending out a search party to catch the beast?"

"I haven't been convinced that it exists. More than half the people in the area report they saw no such thing, only people running."

Nikolai leaned forward on his throne, peering intently at Lukas. "Well, of course, there's a dragon."

Lukas's mouth went dry, and it took a second before he spoke. "But I thought you didn't want to hear talk of dragons."

"I didn't want to hear the foolishness Galileo's always running on about. Now the people can see for themselves that dragons are cruel and dangerous."

The familiar cold glint returned to his uncle's eyes. "Ready the forces to deal with this threat. Send out a search party to scour the area. My treasurer will be notifying the citizens of the additional taxes we will be collecting to pay for this force. We shall call them dragon taxes. Think old Galileo will appreciate that?"

The chancellor grinned like a boy playing king as he gave his orders. This version of his uncle scared Lukas more than the harsh one. He saluted and backed out of the room.

His father was waiting for him when he returned home.

"How did he take it?" Stephan asked without preamble.

Lukas shook his head. "Too well. He's convinced the dragon exists and has instructed me to hunt for it."

"Can the disappearance of the man be associated with your missing soldiers?" his mother asked.

Lukas plopped down at the table, and Stephan placed food in front of him and Melea.

"I thought of that. It can't be a coincidence, but a dragon? Really?" He shoveled food into his mouth without taking the time to taste it.

"Why is that more unlikely than nine soldiers deserting all at once with no cause?" she said.

Stephan joined them at the table. "What are you going to do?"

"Put together a search party. But I have no idea how to search for a dragon. What do I look for?"

"Have you asked Galileo?" his mother said.

"I tried, but the healer put him on bedrest. I can't see him right now."

"Oh, poor Ashton. She'll be juggling the store and caring for her grandfather. You should take her some venison stew. It will strengthen the old man and give her one less thing to think about," she said.

"Ashton's gone."

"What?" Melea and Stephan exclaimed together.

"Not disappeared—gone. She went somewhere. I don't know where or why. She didn't tell me; the healer did."

Neither of his parents spoke.

"Father, will you take over the training of the soldiers? I have other tasks for Raquel."

"Of course."

Melea swirled the liquid in her cup as she spoke. "Galileo has always been sure dragons existed. Maybe there's something in the palace archives that can help you track them down."

He turned the suggestion over in his head. "Brilliant idea, Mother!" Lukas kissed her on the cheek. "I'll go there right now."

He dashed out the door, jittery with anxious energy finally released toward a purpose. He tried to cobble together a plan of action that would be most efficient. His first stop had to be the palace scholar who had given him lessons.

Lukas pounded on the door for a solid minute before the tall, slender woman opened the door.

"Master Gena, I need your help."

"Sir Lukas, both suns have set. Can't this wait until morning?"

"It can't. I won't take long."

She stepped aside and let him enter.

"I'm in need of palace records referring to the dragons."

Gena inhaled sharply.

"Is there a problem?" he asked.

She took her time answering, carefully making her way to the sitting room. "Why are you looking for those records?"

"The chancellor has commanded me to hunt down the dragons to stop them from causing any more problems for Olmerta."

"The chancellor, you say?"

"Yes. Is there a problem?"

"No problem." She considered her words carefully. "It's been a long time since anyone besides

Galileo spoke of dragons. It's not something the palace takes lightly."

"Perhaps you haven't heard. One was spotted today in the square."

Gena's face lit up. She appeared to get taller before his eyes.

"The records you seek are very old. No one has been in that section of the vault for many generations. I have never seen them, only heard tales passed from scholar to scholar," the master said. "Even we have not been allowed to venture there . . . but if the chancellor requires it . . ." The unspoken question hung in the air.

"I would welcome your help," Lukas said quickly. "As you know, history was never my strong suit."

"Wait here. I will gather some things to aid us." Master Gena walked with a spring in her step and came back quickly with a bundle she shoved into Lukas's arms. She left through another door, reappearing moments later, carrying a basket weighted down with objects.

"Let's go." By the front door, she picked up a lit lantern. "Grab the other one. I don't suspect there will be light where we're going."

Chapter 14

The wooden door creaked on its hinges when Lukas shouldered it open. The stale air smelled slightly of damp earth and coarse sleeping hides. It registered somewhere in the back of his mind that the book covers may have been made from the same animal skins as his outdoor gear.

Master Gena stepped in, holding her lantern high. The light didn't penetrate to the far reaches of the cavern. Two thick wooden tables lightly coated with dust were arranged in the middle of the room. Lukas ran his fingers over the surface of one.

"Once the vault was declared off-limits, I suspect the seal on the door kept the daily dirt and grime from accumulating," Gena said. She placed her basket and lantern on a table, then pulled out clean parchment, a pen, and an inkpot.

"I do hope your penmanship has improved," she said.

He let the comment slip by without a response. Taking in the rows and rows of shelves, he asked, "Where do we begin?"

"I'm not sure," she answered. "I've never been down here. I've only heard of its riches. Let's scan the shelves and see if we can figure out the old masters' method of organization."

They each took a light and started at opposite ends of the vault, searching the shelves closest to the tables first.

Unbound pages were shelved next to bound tomes gilded in gold. Some stood on end, proudly displaying their spine, while others were stacked on top of each other. Lukas quickly got lost in the many titles promising battle reports and visiting dignitaries.

"I found something," Gena called from halfway down the third row.

Lukas joined her as she carefully placed the open book on the table. He looked over her shoulder where her finger traced the scrawled handwriting.

"What queen?" Lukas asked, the words jumping off the page at him. "We never had a queen."

Gena ignored him and kept reading. When she turned the page, a charcoal drawing of a woman in britches and a long cape captured his attention. But it wasn't the crown on her head that was so unusual; it was the massive head of the large beast she was face to face with that took his breath away.

The master scholar touched the paper reverently. "She's beautiful."

Indeed, although the drawing was in black, white, and grays, somehow the artist had captured the essence of the two creatures so their figures almost glowed.

"Who are they?" Lukas asked in a whisper.

Gena squinted and moved her face closer to the page to make out the writing. "It's smudged. I can't tell. Looks like a Br."

"Brindisi," Lukas said.

She looked from the page to Lukas. "How do you get that?"

"Brindisi is Galileo's dragon. The one in his shop he refuses to sell."

"It may end in an I. The other is only identified as the Queen of Olmerta."

"Turn the page. What else does it say?"

Gena turned the page, and they read together. Most of the text was vague and hard to decipher.

Finally, Lukas walked away in exasperation. "I don't understand. How did we go from a queen and partnership with dragons to where we are today?"

Master Gena leaned back in her seat and watched him pace. "Things are never as simple as a straight line."

"What's that supposed to mean?" Lukas asked.

"It might not be a simple answer—to tell you how we went from a queen to a chancellor."

"I'll bet the chancellor knows," Lukas said sourly.

Master Gena studied him. "It's probably not a question you want to ask."

"Let's see what other secrets are trapped within these walls," Lukas said. He picked up his lantern and went to the area Gena had found the open book. She followed.

He quickly got frustrated with the boring titles on the dusty volumes and wandered deeper into the stacks. While Gena pulled out pages to investigate, Lukas went as far as he could into the cavern and started poking around. He used his free hand to open a selection of crates and examine their contents.

"There's a chest back here," he called out.

Gena joined him and caught his lantern before it spilled over in his haste to pry off the lid.

"Hand me that light." His voice was a command, not a request.

Master Gena did as he bid.

The light glinted off the brilliant gold crown nestled in the bed of straw. Both froze at the sight.

"This makes it real, doesn't it?" Lukas reached in and picked up the crown encrusted with royal blue sapphires.

"It's amazing," Gena said. "I wonder who wore it last."

Lukas tilted it this way and that, catching the light. "I wonder who's supposed to be wearing it now."

Through unspoken agreement, they moved back to the books, but Lukas carried the crown with him.

As they worked through the volumes, Gena took notes to important references about the dragons. No one volume contained all the answers, so they knew they would be piecing things together. Some of the stories seemed to be imaginary, written for young children or as part of the primers used to teach reading. It was hard to separate the possibly real from the probably made-up.

Gena unwrapped the bundle Lukas had carried into the cavern. Bread, cheese, and a wineskin kept them nourished through their search. They had been at it for hours when they heard pounding from the entryway.

Four soldiers poured into the space, lanterns and swords equally balanced.

"What's the meaning of this?" Lukas called.

"Sir Lukas, the chancellor has ordered these doors shut."

"I'm here under the chancellor's orders," he replied.

"Sir, I beg you. The chancellor has ordered us to clear these premises immediately."

Master Gena started gathering their items.

"You'll have to leave those behind, Master," a soldier said.

"Don't be ridiculous. Leaving food down here will only attract vermin. We can't have that." She continued placing things in her bag.

"Take the food then, but no books or papers shall leave this vault, by order of the chancellor."

While Lukas protested, Gena packed their things. She left the notes she had taken on the table. "Let's go, Sir Lukas. We can address this with the chancellor at a later date. These soldiers are doing their duty."

Lukas marched off in anger. While the research hadn't answered all his questions, they were at least making headway.

At the top of the steps, the guards relayed a final message to Lukas. "The chancellor has requested your company in his throne room."

Master Gena implored him. "Go see the chancellor. Explain we are sorry to report we found nothing to help us in his effort to track down the dragons."

Lukas hesitated, but she gave him a gentle push. "I'm sorry I couldn't be of further assistance to you."

As the soldiers escorted him away, his mind spun with the thoughts of queens and dragons.

"What were you doing in the vault? They are sealed for a reason," Nikolai snapped.

Lukas stood at attention before his uncle, a position he was getting pretty tired of. "Sir, you ordered me to hunt the dragons. I was looking for clues where to start."

"I would have thought you would have started with that old fool."

"Sir, Galileo has taken ill. He isn't in any position to help."

Nikolai barked out a harsh laugh. "Serves the old man right. As soon as his precious dragons reappear, the people discover they aren't everything he has been claiming."

The chancellor rested his chin on his fist. "What did you find in the vault?"

Lukas's mind raced along with his heart. "Dusty tomes, sir. Mostly records of trade with neighboring villages. Pretty boring actually," he added as an afterthought.

"How did you get in?"

"I ordered the Master Scholar to assist me. She discouraged my search, but when I insisted, she went with me to ensure I didn't damage any of the books."

Nikolai gave him a skeptical look and held out his hand. "Give me the key."

"The key?"

"Don't play dumb. It doesn't look good on a member of my family. The key to the vault."

Lukas pulled the key from his pocket and reluctantly handed it over.

"There's nothing in the vaults to help you." Nikolai placed the key in the inner pocket of his jacket. "You should be focused on finding those creatures before they wreak more havoc on Olmerta."

"My soldiers are still conducting interviews and searching for clues."

"You need to lead the charge. The people need to see the Cabots coming to their rescue. For too long, they have revered Galileo's pets."

Although Lukas had his doubts about dragons, the insults about Galileo didn't sit right with him. "I will find the dragons, Uncle. You can count on me."

"Bring me the head of a dragon. These stupid people want to adorn their homes with dragons; let me adorn the city gates with its carcass."

Lukas bowed slightly at the waist with his palm on his heart. His mouth was dry, so no words came out.

Chapter 15

Ashton and Sheba forged ahead at a fast walk through the dim forest. After being chased, the unnatural silence weighed heavily on her. She took her bow from where it hung from Sheba's saddle and pulled an arrow from the quiver on her back. Lukas's sword was in its place at her belt; hopefully, she wouldn't encounter anything at close range so that she'd need to wield it.

She kept her ears tuned to any sound of movement. Hours passed as they made their way through the endless woods, and the heightened state started to take a toll on Ashton. She rolled her shoulders, trying to loosen her tight muscles. She made circles with her head, relaxing her neck.

Now that the adrenalin had worn off, the need for food and water made her head hurt. She pulled a hunk of bread from her pack along with a waterskin. She didn't want to think about who may have been following her or why they had given up. The natural insect sounds of the forest had gradually returned, along with an occasional screech of a large bird.

Trying to put the unseen trackers out of her mind, she carried on a one-way conversation with

Sheba, asking how she got along with Zephyr and the other horses in the village. When that didn't seem to help, she sang songs her mother taught her years ago. Anything to keep frightening thoughts at bay.

The distractions made her feel better, and the sense of eyes following her lessened. She found herself almost enjoying the ride. After several more hours, she was getting hoarse from singing and reached again for her waterskin.

Ahead, light filtered through the treetops, beckoning her. Without prodding, Sheba picked up her pace.

A sudden crash off to her right drew Ashton's attention seconds before Sheba reared up on her hind legs. Focusing on the precarious grip on her horse, Ashton could only sense dark figures running across their path, spooking Sheba further. Tree branches whipped across Ashton's face as Sheba came down on all fours, then reared again.

Minutes passed before Ashton was able to get control of Sheba and calm her down. Whatever had spooked the horse was gone; the only sound now was Ashton's heartbeat and the heavy breathing of the horse. She rested her head on Sheba's neck and willed her heart to slow.

When she stopped trembling, she nudged Sheba forward.

Emerging from the canopy, they came upon a pebbly clearing as large as the Olmerta town center, ending at the edge of a deep ravine. No green poked through the small stones, but there was beauty in the way they winked in the sunlight. Ashton slid off Sheba's back and took in the golden canyon below. The pace of the river in the distance reached her ears like a hush. The sand along the banks glittered and reflected yellow from the bushes and trees lining the ravine floor.

She couldn't think of a time when she had seen so many yellow leaves on trees in full bloom. When the wind blew, some leaves turned, showing their orange underside. It was mesmerizing.

Ashton looked up and down the length of the crevice but saw no way to cross. She might have to go down and climb back up, but no path presented itself. The trees from the forest behind her grew thickly right up to the edge on both sides of the clearing. The ground looked ready to give way under them at any time while their roots clung tightly.

Hating the idea of turning away from the beauty and light of the ravine, she notched an arrow in her bow and led Sheba back into the darkness to look for another path.

As her eyes adjusted to the light, Ashton heard something large moving toward her with some speed. Without thinking, she raised her bow and fired. She held her breath and reached for another arrow, waiting to hear whether the creature fell or continued forward.

"Guess you owe me five more brakons," Lukas said.

"Maybe I was aiming for the tree."

"Yeah, that's it." Lukas and Zephyr approached. "Will you point that thing somewhere else? You might get lucky and hit me."

She lowered the bow but didn't put it away. "What are you doing here?"

"Out for a ride."

Lukas's broad smile melted Ashton. It was good to see him.

"How did you know where to find me?" she asked.

"It wasn't easy. It wasn't as if you left me a note."

"I didn't expect you to come looking."

"I went by the shop. You need to fix the broken latch on the back door, by the way. What happened there? It looks like you were looted."

"No, Galileo had a run on items in the store. Then the dragon came."

"You saw the dragon?"

"Of course. How could I miss it? It flew into the center of town."

"Not everyone saw it."

"What are you talking about? It was huge."

Lukas shook his head. "I'm telling you. We interviewed everyone. Half saw it; half didn't. It was the weirdest thing."

Ashton tried to make sense of it. "But what does that have to do with you following me?"

"I found piles of papers on the counter in the shop."

"Grandfather and I were going through them to find information about the dragons."

"You left the map on the top of the pile. I thought you meant it for me." He pulled a page from inside his tunic and leaned over in his saddle to hand it to her.

Ashton stared at the notations. It wasn't anything special.

"Turn it over."

On the reverse side, a topical map was drawn in black ink. In the center was a mountain with dark clouds around its peak. Symbols for trees and rivers were clear, along with other symbols that meant nothing to her.

"What's this?" she said, pointing to a spot on the map.

"It's how we mark no-go zones for patrols. Dangerous spots to be avoided."

She studied the map closer. "Isn't that where we are?"

"Yep."

She shuddered. "Glad I didn't see this before. I might have thought twice before entering this creepy forest."

"If you never saw the map, that means you didn't mark this spot as your destination?" He indicated a red circle around the mountain.

She shook her head.

"Then why did you come this way?"

She thought long and hard before answering. Grandfather had told her to beware of the Cabots. But Lukas had been her friend forever. Surely her grandfather didn't distrust Lukas as he did his uncle.

She tempered her response. "Not one specific thing. I knew I had to do something. I can't say I had a plan when I started. I felt a . . . calling. I can't explain it."

"Like a pull?"

"Yeah, like that. And Sheba seemed to know the way."

"I felt it too. I thought it was tied to this." He reached inside his pants pocket and pulled out her blue leather book. "You must have dropped this along the path."

Frantically, Ashton searched her pockets as if there could be another blue leather book. Finding nothing, she took it from Lukas. "Where was it?"

"At the base of the foothills. Looks like you made camp there."

"I did. But I swear I had it with me when I began this morning. I didn't leave anything behind."

"Except me."

She looked at him seriously. "You didn't seem interested in my dragon hunt."

"I'm sorry for that. I was an ass. It was uncalled for."

She waved it away. "Thanks for finding my book."

"I don't see what the big deal is. It's nothing but gibberish."

"You looked in the book?"

"Well, I peeked. I wanted to see if it was yours. None of the words made sense though. If it weren't for the symbol on the cover, I wouldn't have even thought it was yours."

Ashton opened it and looked through it. It was the same book her grandmother had left her. "I didn't know your reading was so bad. It's not gibberish."

He laughed out loud. "You're pulling my leg. You had me going with the whole male dragons laying eggs thing."

She turned the page toward him. "You can't read this?"

"Of course not, and neither can you."

She read, "Dragons particularly like relaxing in the hot afternoon just before the first sun sets. Their favorite spot is beside the lake where the sand has soaked up the heat from the day."

"Very funny."

"Lukas, I'm not joking. This is clear to me."

He stopped smiling. "Let me see."

She handed him the book, and he flipped through the pages. "Nope. All scribbles to me."

"Interesting." Ashton took the book, looking at it one more time before placing it inside her tunic.

"But the feeling of being pulled started once I picked it up. Somehow, I knew it was yours. I followed my instincts—and Zephyr's. It wasn't like you were hiding your tracks."

"What about the circle of trees? How did you know where to enter on the other side?"

"You mean across the meadow? There was only one way in and one way out the other side. It didn't take a lot of deduction."

"Did anyone try to stop you?"

"Like who?" Lukas asked. "No one lives in these woods."

Ashton was confused but didn't feel like taking the time to explain. Instead, she pointed over her shoulder to the end of the path. "I was trying to figure out a way across the ravine. I'm doubling back to see if there's a way around."

Lukas nudged Zephyr past Ashton, the sides of the horses bumping in the confined space. By degrees, Ashton slowly turned Sheba to follow.

Lukas looked out over the deep crevice. "You didn't trust the bridge?"

"What bridge?"

"The one that crosses the ravine." He paused for a moment to study her face. "What's gotten into you?"

Attaching the bow to the saddle, Ashton dismounted and walked to the edge. A large wooden bridge with woven rope sides traversed the gorge, attached to large oak trees on both sides. It looked in good repair and was easily wide enough for the horses and a small wagon.

"I swear it wasn't there before."

"Looks like it's been here a long time to me." Lukas climbed off Zephyr and tugged on the bridge's supporting ropes. There was no give. "Seems to be safe though. No signs of fraying."

Ashton sat on the hard ground. She felt confused and a little frightened. No way could she have missed the bridge before.

"Are you okay?" Lukas squatted in front of her. He put a hand on her forehead, then her cheek.

She only looked at him. With the bright sky behind him and the golden glow coming up from the valley, an odd aura surrounded his head and shoulders. She shoved him, and he fell on his backside.

"Hey, what was that for?"

"I needed to see if you were real."

"Ashton, honestly, what's up with you? Did you take a fall? Hit your head? You don't seem to have a fever."

"Something isn't right. That bridge wasn't here before."

"Maybe you were too busy taking in the valley below. Gorgeous, isn't it? What kind of trees are those?"

Ashton knew he was trying to distract her. Get her mind on something else so she wouldn't think about being crazy. She stood up and searched the ground for a large rock. Collecting several, she walked to the bridge and tossed one onto the wood planks. It rattled and thunked before settling a few horse-lengths in.

Then she threw one as far as she could. It hit the bridge with a crack, then bounced over the edge.

Lukas walked a few steps onto the bridge and jumped up and down. "Satisfied?"

She tossed a rock up in the air and caught it while she thought. "Let's go."

Chapter 16

Taking the reins in her hand, she led Sheba to the bridge. The mare resisted and shied away from the edge. Ashton spoke soothing words to her as she stroked her nose. Lukas was behind her doing the same thing for Zephyr.

As they made their way across, Ashton was surprised at how still the bridge was. Although she felt a breeze on her face, the suspended walkway didn't sway. Even the heavy footsteps of the horses didn't cause movement.

It wasn't until they were across and standing on firm ground that she spoke to Lukas again. "Did that seem odd to you?"

"I wish we could build bridges like that," he said at the same time.

They laughed together, and the sound cheered her immensely.

The forest ahead was green and lush. The treetops overlapped, but it wasn't thick enough to block out the sun. Dappled light illuminated the variegated shades of the ground cover.

The grass on this side of the bridge was thick, so Ashton and Lukas allowed their horses to graze.

She reached into her pack and handed Lukas a round fruit, taking another for herself.

"I don't suppose you thought to bring food," she said.

"I did, actually." He reached into his pack and brought out beef jerky and nuts.

"Don't eat that unless you brought along a lot of water to wash it down."

He looked sheepish. He shook his waterskin, already half empty. "I have one extra."

She smiled, pulling out her water. "Thanks for coming after me. Isn't your uncle going to have a fit when he realizes you're gone?"

Lukas took a large bite from the fruit and crunched. "He's expecting me to be gone. He told me to hunt down the dragon."

Ashton froze. "You followed me hoping I'd lead you to the dragon?"

"Well, you and Galileo know more about dragons than anyone. What else would you think was more important than your grandfather's health?" He shrugged. "I figured you were trying to find the dragon. Your grandfather's improving, by the way." He took another large bite.

She was no longer hungry. A sick feeling in her stomach replaced her relief at seeing Lukas. Maybe this was what her grandfather warned her about.

Lukas must have sensed a change. "What's wrong? You've gone white."

Her mind was reeling. "There's something more going on here that we don't understand. I can't believe the dragons are here to hurt us."

"Tell that to the guy who got carried off in the middle of his family outing." Lukas walked over to where Zephyr was grazing and fed her the core of his fruit.

When he turned around, Ashton was gathering Sheba's reins, preparing to mount. "Okay, guess we're ready to go."

"I am," Ashton said. "You can go to your uncle. I'm not about to help you hunt down and kill the dragons."

"Who said anything about killing?"

"The chancellor isn't trying to make nice with them. He has a different agenda."

Lukas grabbed Sheba's bridle, holding Ashton in place. "I am not my uncle." His face was so stern, Ashton had to look closely to see he wasn't acting.

"What's your plan?" she asked, steel in her voice.

"I came to find you. If the rumors are true, these beasts are real, and I don't want you facing them alone. Why is that so wrong?"

"I don't need a spy from the palace. Do you have troops following us? Waiting to swoop in once we clear the way?"

"Don't be ridiculous. I'm here on my own. No one else is stupid enough to enter the danger zones."

"So now I'm stupid." Ashton pulled at Sheba's reins, trying to free her head from Lukas's grip.

"Well, when you act like this you are. Stop it."

She sagged in the saddle, tired already of fighting. "I want to figure out what's going on. There has to be a reason a dragon has returned, and there has to be a reason it's attacking."

"Frankel may not be its first kill. Mother suggested a dragon attack would explain my missing soldiers."

"That's awful. But it's even a better reason to find the queen dragon and figure this out."

"What queen dragon?" he asked.

Ashton leaned forward and patted Sheba, avoiding looking at Lukas. "Grandfather said only the queen can stop them."

"Them?"

"I don't know. The dragons, I guess."

"What are you going to do when we find her? Have a cup of tea and discuss politics? What will you accomplish?" Lukas walked away from Sheba and mounted Zephyr.

Ashton stewed in annoyance. They had entered the green forest before she bothered to respond.

"From the things written in my book, humans and dragons must have had some way to communicate. How else would they know all the details recorded there?" she said.

"I'll take your word for it. That doesn't mean you'll be able to talk to them."

"I'll figure it out," she said.

They rode in silence.

Ashton smelled the moisture in the air long before she heard the roar of the water crashing onto rocks. The leaves on the trees grew larger and brighter the closer they got to the edge of the forest. As they left the woods, a lush garden of flora spread before them.

"It looks like the picture in my book," she whispered.

Sliding off Sheba's back, she walked alongside her mount to the water's edge. Zephyr and Lukas joined them. The horses sniffed the pooling water, then drank in the cool freshness.

Both Lukas and Ashton followed, getting down on their knees to scoop the water with their hands. After quenching their initial thirst, they refilled their waterskins.

"The second sun has almost set. We should probably camp here tonight," Lukas said.

"I wonder how much further we have to go."

"Doesn't that book tell you?"

"There's no spot marked 'dragons are here,' if that's what you're asking. So far, I've been following where the trail leads."

Lukas looked around. "I don't see a trail out of here."

She agreed. "We can scout around in the morning. Maybe it'll be more obvious in full light."

Rushing to finish before losing the sun, they tended to the horses, removing their saddles and brushing out their coats. The horses wandered as Lukas and Ashton gathered sticks for a small fire. Ashton carried over a larger log half-eaten by insects. They cleared the ground to make a fire circle and laid out the wood but didn't light it right away.

As the sun set, bright dots filled the sky. Lukas lay on his bedroll and crossed his hands on his stomach. "I forgot the stars were this bright."

Ashton laid down with her head close to his but her feet pointing in the opposite direction. She wiggled to get comfortable, brushing aside rocks to make a smoother surface. Something sharp poked her in the side, and she tossed it toward the fire.

The insects grew louder as Lukas and Ashton got quieter. Nearby, the swish of a tail brushing away annoying flying bugs was the only sign of movement.

"If I had known the path led here, I might have come much earlier," Ashton said wistfully.

"Seems like a great place to build a house."

Ashton cleared her throat. "Like when you get matched?"

"Why are you in such a hurry to marry me off? I'm hoping Uncle Nikolai forgets about it altogether."

"But a match with a neighboring village could mean a lot. You'll eventually be chancellor when your uncle dies, unless he has some children we don't know about. Making alliances is part of the job description, isn't it?"

He harrumphed. "How would you feel about it if you didn't have a say in the person you'd spend the rest of your life with?"

She felt her face grow hot. "It wouldn't be my first choice, but if it's good for the village . . ."

"Then *you* marry someone from Melak. I'll give you an official title, and you can secure the alliance."

"If that's what you wish, Chancellor Lukas." She got up to start the fire.

He gave a mirthless laugh, still staring at the night sky. "Marrying you off would be like giving away half of myself."

She kept her face averted from him while she stoked the fire.

He let out a deep breath. "I don't want to be chancellor. Neither does my father."

"Either one of you could do better than Nikolai. At least your dad stands up for the villagers against your uncle."

Lukas sat up and stared as the fire took hold of the kindling. "My father was even more outspoken before Roland died."

Ashton risked a glance at Lukas but didn't say anything.

"Roland was next in line. He would have been a great chancellor. He was a lot like my father."

"So are you," Ashton said.

Lukas went on as if he hadn't heard her. "The palace guards told my parents it was a training accident, but it felt much more personal."

He threw a stick into the flames. "I heard people whispering about the real cause, but my father never insinuated the death was anything but the will of the gods."

96

The silence hung between them as Ashton tried to think of something to comfort him.

"Not only did I lose my brother, but my father changed overnight. He was a beaten dog around Nikolai, constantly warning me to keep my opinions to myself. I know something happened to Roland, and I can't believe it was an accident."

He laid back down with his hands behind his head, lost in his thoughts.

Unrolling her bedroll, she busied herself settling in. Once she was comfortable with her back to the fire, she spoke. "Lukas, I'm glad you're here."

"Ashton, I'm glad you didn't shoot me."

Chapter 17

"I see you," said the voice.

Ashton sat up and looked around. The fire still glowed faintly, enough to black out anything outside its immediate ring. Lukas was fast asleep, one arm covering his eyes.

"Your grandfather has taught you well, but you have so much more to learn," the voice continued.

Could it be? Ashton didn't want to hope. "Grandmother? Is that you? Where are you?"

Lukas stirred in his sleep. Ashton reached over and poked him, trying to wake him without scaring off the voice.

"He's not ready, but he'll come around. You've chosen wisely with that one."

Ashton pulled her hand away as if burnt. She moved her head from side to side, trying to catch movement with her peripheral vision. The voice chuckled.

That was not her grandmother's laugh. Suddenly she recognized she was very vulnerable on the ground. She felt for her sword and picked it up as she stood.

"What do you want?"

"To communicate. Isn't that what you were hoping for?"

"Then step into the light so I can see you."

"You aren't close enough yet, but you're on the right path."

"Close enough to what?"

Only silence answered her.

"We need to get going." Lukas nudged her with his foot. "I let you sleep as long as I could."

Ashton sat up slowly, the feeling of déjà vu overtaking her. Lukas handed her a waterskin. "Drink. Let's go."

She took the skin and downed it. He handed her some salted meat. "Figured we can eat this while we have plenty of water."

She took it and chewed without speaking.

"What's up with you?" he asked as he went about clearing their site. Dumping water on the coals sent up a white puff of smoke with a hiss.

She got to her feet and wandered into the woods to relieve herself. Then she went to the river to splash water on her face and refill her waterskin.

When she got back, Lukas had finished. "Did you have strange dreams last night?" she asked him.

He thought for a moment. "I didn't dream at all. I slept soundly though. Is that your problem? Did you have a bad dream?"

"Not bad exactly, but strange. I heard a voice."

"Did it tell you to defend yourself? You were gripping your sword hilt when I woke up. I took it away from you." He pointed to Sheba, who was already saddled and ready to ride. Ashton's sword belt hung from the horn.

"Tell me about it on the ride. How much farther do you think we have to go to find these dragons of yours?" he asked.

"I have a feeling they'll find us when they're ready." She climbed into the saddle and guided Sheba downriver to find a shallow place to cross.

Lukas rode up beside her. "What do you make of this?" He handed her a curved piece of bone about the size of her hand. "I found it when I was dousing the fire."

She turned it over. One end of the curve came to a point, while the other ended in a flat, thick base. "It looks like a tooth."

"Not from anything I've ever seen," he said.

She handed it back to him.

"Are you still feeling that pulling sensation?" Lukas asked.

She paused. "I am, but it's very subtle." Abruptly, she turned Sheba's head toward their campsite.

"Where are you going?" Lukas asked.

"Experimenting." She rode toward the woods they had traveled through the day before. As they got closer, Sheba slowed her pace. When she came to a standstill, Ashton gave a tap with her heels. Sheba wouldn't move. Ashton relaxed the reins and gave Sheba her head. The horse turned and cantered to where Lukas sat, confused.

"Did you forget something?" he asked.

"We aren't the only ones feeling the pull. The horses sense it as well. Sheba wouldn't go into the woods." Ashton continued along the river.

"Well, let's hope the pull isn't like a fisherman reeling in a catch. I don't feel like being someone's dinner."

100

"I don't think that's the plan."

A hot breeze hit their backs, causing the horses to break into a run. Ashton grabbed the saddle to keep from falling off with the sudden change of speed. Once balanced, she glanced over her shoulder to see a dark shadow cover the ground. The green bulk quickly overtook them and cut off their path.

"What the—" Lukas exclaimed as Ashton guided Sheba into Zephyr, pushing her toward the trees.

"Under cover! Now!" she shouted.

They raced for the tree line. The wind buffeted the leaves, causing a rattle as they fought to hold on to their branches. When the horses were far enough in that Ashton felt safe, she pulled Sheba to a halt.

"What's going on?" Lukas asked, out of breath.

"Didn't you see the dragon?"

"Dragon? No. I saw a dark shadow on the ground, then you were off like something was chasing you."

"It was!" She looked him squarely in the eye. "Are you messing with me right now? It wouldn't be a good time."

"I'm not messing with you. I didn't see anything."

She walked Sheba slowly toward the opening in the trees. A yellow, scaly creature swept back and forth in the sky, its wingspan easily six horse-lengths long. Ashton heard a screech and felt the warm wind seep into her clothes.

"Did you hear that?" she called without turning away from the yellow dragon.

"I heard it." Lukas was now beside her, straining to see what she was looking at.

From down river, a steely-blue mass, twice the size of the yellow, hurtled into view. With a quick unfurling of its wings, the dragon seemed to stop in midair and raise its talons to meet the oncoming blue mass.

The smaller couldn't stop in time to avoid the razor-sharp trap. Another screech of fury and pain cut through the trees. Both Lukas and Ashton instinctively covered their ears. In a flash, the blue dragon beat down with its wings, carrying both dragons high into the sky. Before Ashton could get far enough out of the trees to look up, they were gone.

Chapter 18

Carefully, Ashton and Sheba walked into the open.

"Are you going to tell me what's going on?" Lukas asked.

She spun in the saddle to face him. "Are you seriously going to sit there and tell me you didn't see those two dragons fighting?"

He stared at her as if she had gone mad.

"Unbelievable." She kicked her horse into gear and started down river at a trot.

Lukas hurried to follow but gave her some space. "Where are they now?" he eventually asked.

"That's what we're going to find out."

Ashton briefly entertained the idea she was losing her mind, but quickly dismissed it. She knew she saw the dragon—perhaps the same green one—in the town center the day Frankel disappeared.

"Why can't you see them?" Ashton asked, almost to herself. Then it hit her. She pulled Sheba back to a fast walk. "Do you believe in dragons?"

"Believe?"

Ashton had seen Lukas use this stall tactic before when trying to come up with a good answer. She laughed aloud. "You're hunting something you don't believe exists. How do you expect to find them?"

"I came looking for you. My uncle thinks I'm hunting dragons. I didn't say I was."

She smiled. Mincing words was a special art Lukas excelled at. When they got into trouble with Grandfather, she always let Lukas talk their way out of it. "Well, you better start believing, or you might find yourself in deep trouble."

"I'll be honest, when it was solely Galileo's stories, I was skeptical. But with everything that's happened, I'd be wrong not to consider the possibility."

Whether he was ready to hear it or not, Ashton had to trust he'd come around eventually. "There was a rather large green dragon who chased us into the trees. A much larger steely-blue dragon came to our rescue and carried a smaller yellow one away. I think the blue one talked to me last night."

"Talked to you?"

Ashton sighed. As they rode on, she filled Lukas in on her dream, although she wasn't quite convinced it was a dream in the true sense of the word.

When she finished, she gave Lukas time to process everything. "Maybe it's the same reason you can't read the book. You have to believe. It's like the old song says: 'The faithful will see you; come out when you dare.'"

"That's only a ditty to entertain young children," he said.

"But what if it isn't? What if there's something more to it?"

"How does the rest of it go?"

"'When the dark clouds come, return to the sky. No more in hiding, wings on high,'" she recited in a sing-song voice, while Lukas spread his arms to fly like they did when they were little.

Together they continued. "'The faithful will see you. Come out when you dare. There's a mission awaiting. Travel with care.'"

"Wait, aren't we on a mission?" Lukas said.

She shrugged. "Of sorts. I don't think it's referring to us though. The last verse is, 'From mother to daughter, pass it on down. Capture the plunder. Who wears the crown?'"

"I'm such an idiot!"

"No arguments there. Why this time?"

"I haven't told you about my trip to the archives. I was looking to see if anything like the dragon attacks had happened before."

"And?"

"We didn't get very far. Master Gena was helping me go through the records in some secret vault no one is supposed to go in."

It was her turn to look at him as if he had gone crazy.

He rushed on. "No, really. I went to ask her for help. She knew about the vault but had never been in it. She said entry was forbidden. I said I was working on my uncle's orders, so she took me to it." His words tumbled out so fast, Ashton had a hard time keeping up.

"There was no secret password or anything. That was kind of disappointing. But there was a very large lock. Master Gena got a cool-looking key from security. They didn't even know what it was for. We didn't get much done before the guards came and kicked us out. Then they escorted me to see my uncle."

When he took a breath, she laughed at him. "I've never seen you so excited to look at old books."

"It was more than books. I found a crown!" He beamed with pride.

"A crown? In a long-forgotten vault? Why would Olmerta have a crown?"

"Because we used to have a queen! There was a beautiful drawing—you would have loved it—of a woman with a crown on her head talking to a dragon. I thought it was a bedtime story for children until we found the crown. It had blue sapphires, about the color of your eyes."

He stopped talking abruptly.

"And?" she prodded.

"Um, the soldiers came and kicked us out. We had to leave everything behind."

They came to a spot in the river where it looked safe to cross. Lukas went first, with Zephyr's sure footing taking it all in stride. When they reached the other side, Ashton asked, "What did your uncle have to say?"

"He was pretty angry at first. When I explained what I was looking for, he calmed down a bit but told me I couldn't go back there. He took the key from me. Believe it or not, he's happy to support the idea of dragons as long as they're killing people."

"That's awful," she said.

"I agree. I told him we didn't find anything."

"You didn't tell him about the crown?"

"No. He doesn't deserve to see it. Who knows, he might have melted it down or decided he was a king or something. I couldn't stomach that."

"He's your uncle and the chancellor. Didn't you pledge an oath to him?"

"My oath is to protect Olmerta. I'm not sure what he's up to, but it doesn't feel like he's putting the village first."

"What about Master Gena? Did she tell?"

"She didn't have to go with me. Something tells me she wanted to keep the secret too. She said to tell him she was sorry she couldn't help me find anything."

"I never gave her enough credit," Ashton admitted.

"What does it mean?"

"Which part? That was a lot to unwrap."

"Do you think we had a queen at one time?"

"I can only handle one mystery at a time. At least the records showed evidence of dragons. Why wasn't that enough to make you believe?" she asked.

"As I said, I thought it was a child's tale. Then I got sidetracked on the crown."

"With the sapphire stones . . ." she teased.

He blushed. "It was an interesting crown." He shifted uncomfortably in his saddle. "Things happened quickly after that. I got the order to search for the dragon. I checked on Galileo, then came after you."

"Thanks for watching out for him," she said softly. As worried as she was for his health, she was also excited to be out of that village and experiencing new things.

"What do we do if we find these dragons we're looking for?"

"Grandfather has always believed dragons to be our friends. Seems like at least the blue one is. I think we need to go carefully until we can figure out for sure if it's friend or foe."

Chapter 19

"What do you mean she got away?"

The man dressed all in black stood at attention in front of the chancellor. "Her horse jumped the barricade. By the time we were able to follow, another had entered our area."

"Another?" Nikolai sneered. "Two visitors in one day to the Silent Mountain? That's unheard of."

"It was your nephew, Chancellor."

"Lukas?" Nikolai jumped from his seat and paced the floor, five rapid steps in each direction. He stopped suddenly. "Of course! He's hunting the dragon and knew she'd be searching for the dragons. I didn't think he had it in him. Brilliant plan!"

"Your orders, sir?"

Nikolai started, forgetting he wasn't alone. "Leave them. Conduct your regular patrols. No one else enters those woods. Do you hear me?"

The man saluted and retreated from the room.

Nikolai regained his seat.

This could work out better than I'd hoped, he thought.

"Bayard!" he bellowed.

A slight man with greased-back hair emerged soundlessly from a door behind the throne. "Sir." He bowed slightly from the waist.

"Find that brother of mine. See if he knows what his son is up to. And gather a selection of young women of breeding age. It's time to start my legacy."

"Sir." Bayard bowed again and left as quietly as he entered.

Nikolai pulled out the key that hung around his neck. Dangling from the ribbon in his fingers, the key caught the light and sent rays of color dancing about the throne.

Rising from his seat, Nikolai strode out the side door of the large hall, his most trusted personal guard falling in behind him. Without a word, he led them to the entry of the vault locked tight for so long, he barely remembered seeing it as a young boy.

His father had never been interested in old books or records. He was more of a mind to let his wife run Olmerta while he took advantage of the offerings his rank and privilege gave him. Nikolai's uncle had shown him the underground library, but the boy was too young to appreciate the treasures within.

Shortly after their expedition through the stacks of books, his favorite uncle was tried as a traitor and executed while Nikolai was made to stand beside his father on judgment day. Any thought of returning to explore the books and boxes after that was tempered by fear.

Now it was time to face that fear. As chancellor, it was his right to go where he pleased, and he decided today was the day to revisit the vault.

Standing at the top of the stairs, he paused, taking a deep breath.

"Light that lantern." He indicated one of several lanterns resting on a ledge built into the wall next to the opening. A guard jumped to obey, striking a match to catch on the wick. The immediate result was black smoke that quickly dissolved into yellow light as the guard adjusted the flame. He handed the lantern to Nikolai, then resumed his place in line with the others.

"Wait here. Let no one pass for any reason," he ordered his guard before beginning the descent.

The air had a cloying quality that made it feel hard to breathe. Nikolai loosened the collar of his shirt as he stepped further into the space. The flame inside the glass danced with his movements, causing the shadows to sway and ebb as if alive.

Setting the light on the table next to sheets of parchments and old books, he turned the pages and noted the colors in some of the drawings were breathtaking. He didn't remember seeing anything quite so vibrant in his own library. That would have to change.

Shifting his attention to the loose parchment, he moved them closer to the flame to make out the handwriting. The scratch was that of the palace scholar, written in a language he didn't recognize, although he read and spoke at least three fluently. This was a mixture of symbols he could identify and others that were new to him.

He folded the pages and placed them in the inner pocket of his jacket. Master Gena had some explaining to do. Following the footprints on the dirty floor, Nikolai was able to discern where his nephew and the scholar had searched. He took a quick look at the tomes but was quickly bored.

Ah, what's this? He spied the chests against the farthest wall, almost hidden in the shadows. A few had been recently opened if the disturbed dust was any indication. He lifted the lid on one to reveal gold candlesticks nested in straw, a tarnished dragon wrapped around the base. Dropping the lid, he moved to the next. It contained many smaller boxes. Nikolai set down the lantern so he could study the contents more carefully.

The first box he pulled out held a pair of elegant dragon earrings. The next, a bracelet of finely woven silver. When he moved it closer to the light for inspection, he got the impression of dragon flames moving through the weaves.

"Dragons! Dragons! Dragons! I'm so sick of dragons!" He overturned the chest, boxes tumbling out and glass shattering as it hit the floor. Nikolai kicked the contents for good measure, sending shards skittering across the flagstone.

In disgust, he turned away. Storming up the stairs, he startled his guards when he burst through the doorway.

Chapter 20

"We better make camp," Lukas said.

"It can't be much further," Ashton protested.

"I don't want to run into those things at night. Let's stop here, and we can be at the mountain before the second sunrise." Lukas slid off his horse and unstrapped his saddlebag.

Ashton did the same, removing Sheba's saddle and bit so she could eat freely.

Finished with the horses, Ashton and Lukas gathered firewood and berries without speaking, each lost in their thoughts. Once the fire was lit, the two rested on their bedrolls.

Finally Ashton spoke. "What if Brindisi doesn't exist? What if she's dead or something? Grandfather said to find Brindisi."

Lukas reached over and took her hand. "We'll figure it out. We know the dragons are still around. Let's get to them first, then see what's what."

She squeezed his hand. Her mind was swirling with the many possibilities of what they might find. Eventually she drifted off.

"I see you," came the voice in her mind again.

"Who are you?" Ashton asked in her dream.

"I am who you seek. I'm waiting for you."

"Are you Brindisi?"

A warm caress floated through Ashton's mind, bringing a sense of peace and calm.

"Do you know where my grandmother is?"

The emptiness Ashton suddenly felt was startling in contrast to the recent warmth. She cringed.

"Brindisi?"

Ashton waited for an answer until she finally shifted into a dreamless sleep.

The next morning, Ashton was somber as she went about her tasks.

"Another dream?" Lukas asked.

She nodded without speaking.

As they mounted their horses to start the final leg of their journey, Lukas prodded her. "You can tell me anything, you know."

Without looking at him, Ashton said, "I suspect my grandmother may still be alive."

Lukas stared, waiting for an explanation.

"I found something in Grandfather's papers that makes me believe he was looking for her. I have a feeling she's alive, and he's always known it."

When Lukas didn't respond, she went on. "He took notes, drew maps. He was searching for her, I'm sure of it."

"Why do you imagine it's a person he was searching for and not something else?"

She shrugged. "It's hard to explain. The cryptic notes, the initials used in some places rather than names. He stopped looking when my parents died."

Lukas was silent for several minutes. "So your grandmother has something to do with the dragons?"

"She's the one who left the book for my mother. She must have known about the dragons."

"Why would your parents and your grandfather tell you your grandmother was dead?"

"I couldn't say for sure that I ever heard them say she was dead. I assumed. She was there one day, then gone the next. I remember everyone being sad, but I was so young, I don't remember the details."

Sheba came to a sudden halt, shying away from the path ahead. Ashton looked around for the cause, scanning first the surrounding trees, then the sky. "Lukas, tell me you see that."

"See what? Oh," he said, staring into the sky. "You mean that steely-blue creature with wings? Heading right for us? Yep, I see it. Should we make a run for it?"

Ashton watched the approaching dragon. "I don't think so. It doesn't look like it's on the attack, but it's flying closer."

They both sat very still, watching the blue dragon circle lazily over them three times, then fly away.

"Does it want us to follow?" Ashton asked.

"We don't have a better plan."

They nudged their horses into a walk and kept their eyes on the dragon. After a short while, the dragon landed on a large boulder. Ashton and Lukas approached slowly.

"We're friendly," Lukas said to the massive form waiting for them.

Ashton gave him a funny look.

"What? How am I supposed to know how to talk to a dragon? Did that book say anything about it?"

She had to admit she had no better ideas. She turned to the dragon. "Are you waiting for us?"

The creature unfurled its wings, then tucked them tight again.

"I'm not sure that's an answer," Lukas said under his breath.

"Does that look like an opening under the boulder?" she asked.

He leaned forward in his saddle. "You could be right. It's not big enough for the horses though."

Ashton dismounted and led Sheba under the shelter of the trees. She wrapped her reins around a tree trunk but gave the horse plenty of lead with grasses nearby. Lukas followed behind with Zephyr.

"You ready for this?" Ashton asked him, walking toward the boulder and its sentry.

"I had nothing else planned for today."

When they got closer, the opening in the rock looked smaller than they first figured. "This is great camouflage," he said. "It gets narrow very quickly. It lures an enemy into approaching, only to get stuck when they can't move forward."

"Good thing we aren't the enemy," she said, drawing her sword and pushing ahead into the darkness.

Instead of the musty odor she expected to find inside a cave, Ashton was surprised by the sweet smell that floated to her on a slight breeze. Trailing one hand along the wall to guide her, she moved steadily ahead, not sensing a rise or drop to the ground beneath her. She felt Lukas's hand on her shoulder, assuring her he was there.

As they rounded a bend, a faint light twinkled in the distance. The breeze was stronger now and carried another odor she couldn't place. They walked silently on. Eventually the single light turned into multiple lights. It wasn't until they stepped through the wide opening at the end of the tunnel that the source became apparent.

Inside the large cavern several dragon-lengths high, stretched a lush green meadow of a sort Ashton had never seen. The tall, yellow, reed-like plants swayed in the breeze, which entered the space through multiple holes in the shell of the pyramid. The sunlight streaming through those same portals illuminated large, bush-shaped plants with orange leaves and green berries.

Lukas tapped Ashton and directed her attention to the high ledges secured to the outer walls. Her breath was taken away by the colors of the tremendous beasts resting on the stony outcrop.

"Welcome," a voice sounded. Ashton whipped her head around, trying to locate the source.

"What is it?" Lukas raised his sword in alarm.

"Didn't you hear that?"

"Hear what?"

A soft chuckle sounded in her ear, almost like the purring of a kitten. "He is loyal but not one from your clan."

Lukas started to speak, and Ashton shushed him. She was intent on locating the voice.

"Enter our garden," she heard. "You are secure here as our guests."

Lukas grabbed her arm when Ashton started to move. "Where are you going?" he hissed.

"She says it's okay. Nothing will hurt us here."

"Who?"

"I think it's Brindisi," she said.

"Wise girl," came the voice again.

Ashton took Lukas's hand. "It'll be okay. Trust me." Together they walked into the center of the cavern, feeling the weight of the dragons' eyes on them. Their feet crunching through the shoulder-height grasses was the only sound until a startled roar escaped from the ledge.

Something charged toward them with great speed.

Chapter 21

Before either could process the figure running toward them, the man wrapped his grungy arms around Ashton and lifted her off the ground. He swung her in a circle, smiling broadly.

"I'm so grateful to see you!" the man cried.

Ashton was overwhelmed by the greeting. Lukas tapped the man with the flat of his sword.

"Oh, I'm sorry," the man stammered. He set Ashton on her feet and stepped away. "I never thought I'd see another human again."

"Wait! You're the man from the marketplace, aren't you?" she said.

"Frankel?" Lukas asked.

Frankel nodded vigorously. "Have you seen my family? Are they okay?"

"Your family is fine. My soldiers checked in on them right after the attack. Sad, of course. And confused. They weren't expecting an attack, then they saw the dragon take you," Lukas said.

"How did you get here?" Ashton asked.

"They brought me." He pointed to the beasts on the ledge. "I can't believe I'm in one piece. I thought for sure I was going to be a dragon snack."

"Why did they take you?" Lukas asked.

"I have no idea. I remember being pulled into the sky, then I woke up in this meadow."

"And they haven't told you why you're here?" Ashton asked.

Frankel looked at her skeptically. "How exactly would they tell me?"

Her face got hot, and she turned crimson. "I don't know," she backtracked. "Maybe they can communicate somehow."

"If so, it's not with me. They left me piles of food. When I got hungry enough, I assumed it wasn't poisonous and gave in. These green berries are wonderful." He plucked a handful from a nearby bush and handed them to Lukas.

"But when I try to go through the tunnel you came in, they block my path. Apparently they aren't ready to kill me, but I can't leave either." His face was suddenly crestfallen. "Maybe you're trapped in here now too."

"What else is in here?" Lukas asked.

Frankel led them the way he had come. "Plants very similar to firs grow here; they're purple though. The boughs make for a soft place to sleep. I've kind of set up camp back here. I didn't know how long I would be here. How long has it been?"

"Only a few days," Lukas said.

Frankel looked up to the ledge. "And when I figure out which of these supersized reptiles crushed my son's dream of seeing a dragon, I'm going to turn him into a carry bag."

"My grandfather always said dragons were our friends. Why would they take you?"

"Is Galileo your grandfather? I have a bone to pick with him. This is nothing like the stories he tells. I don't see their actions as being very friendly."

"They didn't eat you," Lukas pointed out.

"Good point," Frankel admitted. "But I'm still a prisoner. I want to get home. How far are we from Olmerta?"

"We're in the Silent Mountain," Ashton said.

"No one goes to the Silent Mountain and returns," Frankel moaned. He flopped down onto a pile of purple pine-like branches.

"We will," Lukas said. "Stay here. I'm going to see if any other tunnels exist besides the one we came in."

"Nope," Frankel called after him as he began following the wall of the cavern. He turned to Ashton. "I've walked these walls many times in the last few days. The dragons block the only way out."

"There has to be another way. They can't fit through the tunnel we came in." Her eyes searched up and down the walls for an opening large enough for the dragons to come and go. "Do you have any water?"

"Oh, I'm sorry. I should have thought to ask if you needed anything. Give me a minute." Frankel ducked behind some trees and was out of sight.

"Rory will transfer you to me," the voice said.

"Who's Rory?" Ashton asked.

Seconds later, a steely-blue dragon with sparkling scales landed before her. It may have been the same one who led them here, but she couldn't be sure. Swiftly but gently, he closed his claw around her and rose into the air. She let out a yelp as she grabbed the claw to keep from falling.

"Rory is heedful. Put your trust in him," Brindisi spoke into Ashton's head.

He landed on the ledge above where Frankel had made camp. When he released her, he gently nudged her toward the rear wall to ensure she didn't get too close to the edge. Then, with one wing, he indicated an entrance carved into the stone at an angle so it couldn't be seen from the ground.

Ashton looked over the meadow and saw Lukas and Frankel looking around franticly. "Up here!" she called to them.

Their eyes were wide as saucers when they spotted her on the ledge. "I'm fine. I'll be right back."

She turned and faced the large creatures blocking her path. As one, they stepped aside to let her pass. When she entered the tunnel, the light from behind her was cut off as the guards moved back into place.

Unlike the one they entered, this tunnel was large and easily tall enough for the dragons to walk through. The shaft twisted and turned, and she lost track of how far she had gone before it opened into another large cavity.

Where the meadow was full of colors and life, this cave appeared to be made of crystal and ice, but it wasn't cold at all. Patterns formed like rivulets on the walls, the flickering sunlight through narrow openings in the dome ceiling making it flow.

The cavern was larger than the entire palace and courtyard combined. Ashton raised her arm to shield her eyes from the dazzling brilliance of light bouncing off the polished stone floor.

"Welcome, granddaughter of Rosa." The voice was loud and clear, although Ashton was still fairly sure the voice was in her head.

She squinted against the brightness, trying to locate the source of the sound. "How are you talking to me?"

"We say *sentsentia*. You may call it *through the mind*," the voice said.

"Are you Brindisi?" she asked.

121

"You do not have to vocalize your words to talk to me. Think them and I will hear."

Feeling a little silly, Ashton gave it a try. "Does that mean you can read my thoughts all the time?"

She almost felt the soft chuckle. "No. I only hear what you direct at me."

A warm wind blew into Ashton's face. When she looked up, the most beautiful creature she had ever seen stood before her. Standing taller than Galileo's shop, the dragon seemed to be the antithesis of the glittering white stone surrounding her. Her long neck was muscular while looking graceful and delicate at the same time. The lustrous black scales glistened as if the creature had recently emerged from the lake. With her wings extended, the leathery membranes changed color with every movement.

Wait until Galileo sees her! Ashton thought.

"Thank you," the dragon replied in a slow, rhythmic voice.

"Wait a minute," Ashton said with her voice. "I thought you said you couldn't read my thoughts."

"When you shout, even in your mind, I cannot help but hear."

Ashton crossed her arms to keep from reaching out to stroke a wing as the dragon folded them and sat low to the ground.

"Yes, I am Brindisi," the dragon replied after a moment. "You have heard of me."

Ashton started to speak aloud and shifted to *sentsentia* instead. "I've read about you."

"Ah, yes. You have the book."

"You know about Grandma's book?"

"Human memories are not like ours. We are the ones who enchanted it, allowing her family to pass important information from one daughter to the other without it being discovered by unwanted eyes."

As Ashton took in the melodic tone of the dragon's voice, she found herself nodding along. *That's why Lukas couldn't read it.*

"The bridge!" she practically shouted.

"The bridge?" Brindisi responded.

"Did you make the bridge disappear? The one over the ravine?"

Ashton felt the rumbling through her feet and supposed the queen was laughing at her.

"The bridge has been there for many generations. You could not see it because you were not ready."

"Because I didn't have the book? Lukas found it for me in the foothills. I must have dropped it."

"Or perhaps the man was to be a part of your journey," Brindisi suggested. "His feelings for you are strong."

Watching the dragon as she shifted position, Ashton was once again struck by the unexpected splendor of this creature.

"My grandfather has made the most wonderful replica of you, although it doesn't come close to your beauty."

Brindisi dipped her head in acknowledgment. "I have been told much about Galileo. He sounds to be a worthy man."

"He is," Ashton replied automatically. For years she had been defending Galileo to the villagers who thought he was a little crazy. She listened to the voice in her head for any sign of mockery and found none.

"Who told you about my grandfather?"

"Your grandmother."

Ashton looked wildly around the room, waiting for her grandmother to appear.

"I am sorry, child. She is no longer with us."

Although Ashton had thought her grandmother dead for years now, hearing it again caused a pain in her heart. "Was she here?"

"She was." The voice was gentle and soothing, very much like Ashton's grandmother.

"How long—" Her mind stumbled over the words the same as if she were speaking aloud. "How long ago did she die?"

"We have mourned her passing for six cycles now."

When Ashton tilted her head in confusion, Brindisi clarified. "I believe you say months."

The blanket of sadness covered her. She didn't know how she would explain to her grandfather that her grandmother had been alive all these years but hadn't come home.

"Look at me, child," Brindisi said softly.

Ashton looked up into the golden, swirling eyes. Her tears dried before they could fall. Her sadness eased and turned more toward happy memories rather than profound loss.

"Your grandmother was precious to our community. She did much to help us when we needed her most. But she did love and miss you all greatly," Brindisi spoke into her mind.

"Why didn't she come home? Or at least get in touch with us?"

"It is difficult to explain. Our wing of dragons is in danger, and she was helping us."

"Helping? What could my grandmother do for you?"

"Rosa had a special gift for healing."

"I didn't think anything could hurt dragons."

Ashton felt the sorrow emanating from the dragon queen.

124

"If only that were true. My wing has been getting sicker and sicker over time. I am at a loss as to the reason why. It has not helped that some of the younger dragons have begun striking out in their frustration."

"So it *was* a dragon who set fire to the tailor shop!" Ashton cried out.

"I received a report of a fire in the village, but it was not intentional. They were only on a scouting mission. They were trying to attract the attention of the villagers who ignored them."

"The villagers couldn't see them. Many in the village don't believe you even exist. My grandfather has been trying to keep the memory of the dragons alive in Olmerta. The fire only made things worse. Taking Frankel was a huge mistake."

Brindisi bristled at the words, but she kept silent.

Then a thought popped into Ashton's head. "Where are the missing soldiers?"

"Soldiers?"

Ashton stared intently at the large queen. "The soldiers who were taken from their posts. Are they okay? We need to tell Lukas. He's been worried sick about them."

Slowly, Brindisi shook her head. "I know nothing about soldiers. I can check with my wing to see if anyone has seen them."

"Why did you take Frankel?"

"He should not have been taken. Speak with him. We have done him no harm."

"Why is he here?"

"Rory was hopeful your Frankel could help us as your grandmother did. He acknowledged Rory, so Rory brought him to me."

"Can Frankel help you?"

The large head shook slowly back and forth. "No, he is not like you or your grandmother."

"What does that mean?"

"He cannot hear us. We cannot explain what we need."

"What do you need?"

Again, a flurry of emotions rushed through Ashton. She felt the dragon's fear, frustration, and rage.

"Your grandmother was developing a compound to put on our eggs to harden the shells until hatching. That has helped, but it is not enough."

"If Frankel can't help you, why haven't you returned him? His family is frantic."

"Our location must remain secret. We are vulnerable in our current state."

"Does that mean you're planning on keeping us prisoner too?" Ashton asked.

"My wing relies on me. I will do what it takes for our survival."

"Even at my expense and the expense of my people?"

She held her head high, towering above Ashton without standing. "If needed."

"That's ridiculous. How can you expect anyone to help you with that attitude?"

"Would you not do the same? Why are you here?" Smoke flowed from Brindisi's nose as she took in the stubborn woman.

Thoughts of her grandfather lying sick in bed and of the villagers crowding the shop looking for answers bombarded her. She was here to help her people and to stop the attacks.

"No one will help you if they fear you," Ashton finally said.

"Do you speak the truth? Your grandmother spoke of humans acting out of fear of their rulers. How is that different?"

"That's not help; that's servitude. That's not having a choice."

The queen settled down, placing her massive head upon her forelegs. As she closed her eyes, she said, "If the choice is between humans or dragons, dragons will triumph."

"Why does it have to be one or the other?"

Ashton waited in silence. When she realized the dragon wasn't going to say more, she turned on her heels. She made her way down the tunnel and arrived on the ledge overlooking the field sooner than she expected. Lukas was calling her name.

"I'm here," she said.

When Lukas spotted her, relief washed over him. Ashton smiled at the look on his face.

She turned to the beast who had flown her to the ledge. "Can you take me down, please?"

The dragon bowed his head and put out his claw. Ashton stepped on gingerly and wrapped her arms around his leg. In no time, the dragon deposited her beside Lukas and resumed his place on the overhang. Lukas grabbed both her shoulders, inspecting her. "Are you hurt?"

Frankel rushed to her side. "Are you okay? I turned around, and you were gone."

"I'm fine," she assured them. "Had to have a little chat with the queen."

"What queen?" Frankel asked.

She gave him an incredulous look. "How long have you been here? Haven't you seen her? Rather large? Black and sparkly? Sound familiar?"

Frankel looked at her blankly. Indicating the dragons on the ledge, he said, "These are the only creatures who have been keeping me company."

"And they haven't . . . *talked* to you in any way?" Ashton asked.

"No, of course not. Why? Did they talk to you?"

Ashton feared being labeled as crazy as her grandfather, but she had to tell them. "Brindisi spoke into my head," she said as nonchalantly as possible.

The men took in her statement in silence.

Finally, something clicked for Lukas. "Your dreams! They weren't dreams, were they?"

"I don't think so. It was Brindisi calling to me so we'd come looking for her."

"Who is Brindisi?" Frankel asked.

"The queen dragon," Lukas and Ashton said together.

Chapter 22

After Ashton filled them in on her conversation with Brindisi, they went to Frankel's make-shift camp to make plans out from under the watchful eyes of the multitude of dragons.

"Will anyone come looking for us?" Frankel asked.

Lukas shook his head. "No one knows we're here."

"Did you find another way out?" Ashton asked.

"No, Frankel's right. That tunnel is the only way."

"Maybe not." Ashton pointed up. "There's at least one opening off the ledge. Maybe there's more."

"How are we supposed to get up there?" Frankel said.

"Your friends up there aren't going to give us a lift to escape," Lukas said.

Ashton laid on the boughs Frankel had set out for her. "Give me some time to think about it." She closed her eyes and promptly fell asleep.

This time, she knew it was a dream, or rather, a memory.

Her grandmother ran into the cottage where Ashton played on the floor with Lukas. They had made a castle out of blocks and stones they had collected.

The farm animals were carved from wood by Galileo and painted in the bright messy colors only children could put together.

"Galileo, I found it!" Rosa called out in excitement.

"Found what?" Ashton's father stepped into the room, wiping his hands on a towel.

"Oh, you're home. Is Galileo here too?"

"He went to the shop," her father said. "What are you all excited about?"

"The dragons! I found the dragons!" She waved some papers in the air in triumph.

"Dragons?" Lukas and Ashton cried out in unison. They plucked their carved dragons from their places on top of the castle and began flying them around the room.

"Daddy, what sound does a dragon make?" Ashton asked as she landed her dragon atop his foot.

He thought about it, then swooped down and picked her up. "Maybe they sound like this." He tickled her, and she giggled, kicking her little feet furiously.

Lukas joined in and tickled Ashton while her father held her. When he finally put her down so she could catch her breath, her grandmother was gone. Lukas and Ashton put their dragons in place to guard over the castle and went in search of something to water the animals.

The horses! Ashton awoke with a start. It was dark in the valley, and she heard the two men breathing softly nearby.

"Rory? Can you hear me?" Ashton wasn't sure how this whole *sentsentia* worked, but it was worth a shot.

"I hear you," came the deep reply, tinged with wonder and joy.

"We left our horses outside. They need water," Ashton said.

"There is plenty of water nearby."

"They are tied to a tree. They can't get water themselves."

For a long few moments, there was nothing but silence. "You only. The others will stay here to ensure you return."

"I'll return." Ashton stood quietly and stepped over Lukas to get to the opening of the makeshift tent. "I won't even go far. Show me where the water is."

She walked toward the center of the meadow where the steely-blue dragon was already waiting. "How does this work best for you?" she asked him.

She felt a soft rumble of an answer, like a chuckle. He put his front claw out and clenched it to make a protective circle around her. "Your tiny feet don't cause me pain."

In one swift motion, they were up and headed toward an opening in the dome. Ashton was torn between trying to trust this giant and fear of smashing into the rock facing. At the last moment, Rory folded his wings as they shot through the narrow opening into the night sky outside.

As he unfurled his wings, the wind resistance made them drop quickly before Rory gave a mighty flap that had them soaring above the treetops. Ashton's stomach was fighting the adjustment to being this high in the air when Rory spoke.

"There. Do you see the lake?"

Ashton peered through his claws and spotted the moon reflecting off the water below. The lake appeared to be smaller than the one in Olmerta, but she had never seen that one from this perspective.

"Got it," she confirmed.

Rory circled and flew directly to the clearing in front of the cave entrance. When he landed, he relaxed his grip and released her.

Her first few steps were halted as she fought to regain her balance. Again, she felt that soft rumble. It made her smile.

She made her way to the horses, talking to them and apologizing for leaving for so long. She untied their reins and led them in the direction of the lake. It wasn't a long walk, but it was through another part of the forest that blocked the moonlight. When she came to a fork in the path, she hesitated.

"Go to the right," Rory said.

"How can you see me?" she asked, even as she led the horses to the right.

"You're warm."

"Uhmmm, I'm not sure what that means," Ashton said.

"I don't know how else to say it. I see you and your animals."

Ashton came out of the trees and let the horses find their way to the water on their own. She followed after, removing first one saddle and then the other as they drank their fill. She went through their bags, collecting anything that might be helpful inside the mountain.

Rory landed near the trees, far enough away to not spook the horses. Ashton took a brush from one of the bags and began brushing Zephyr.

"You like these animals?" Rory asked.

"Very much. They're like friends I can count on. They help me."

"Do they like you?"

She smiled. "I assume so. They like the food I give them, and the shelter over their heads. My tiny feet don't seem to hurt them either."

She moved to brush Sheba. By now, the horses had enough water and were pulling up grass nearby. "Will they be safe if they stay here?"

Rory dipped his head. "We will leave them."

"Thank you." She finished with the horses and gave them each fruit from the bag. Then she threw a pack over her shoulder and walked to Rory. "I'm ready."

Chapter 23

When Lukas rolled over and opened his eyes, Ashton's place was empty. He sat up in a panic.

"Calm down. I'm right here," Ashton said from her place under the canopy strung up between some trees.

Lukas rubbed his hands over his face and joined her. "What are you working on?"

"I got this stuff from our saddle bags. I'm trying to see if any of it helps us."

"Wait—how did you get our saddle bags?"

"Rory took me outside," she said absently as she searched the contents strewed out on the grass in front of her.

Lukas took her arm, forcing her to look up. "Tell me what's going on. You can't go off with these beasts without telling us. What if something happened to you?"

Frankel walked up to them with an armful of various fruits from the meadow. He had a full waterskin over his shoulder.

He knelt and dumped the provisions in front of them. "Breakfast."

Lukas's stomach growled. He picked up a pink, oblong fruit.

When he hesitated, Frankel said, "Go ahead. It's like a peach . . . sort of. Not as sweet, but more filling. Don't eat the skin."

Lukas peeled away the skin that was like layers of leaves. As he worked, he spoke to Ashton. "Tell us how you got out."

"You got out? Why did you come back? You should have made a run for it. You could have brought help for us," Frankel said.

She shook her head. "We can't outrun dragons. Besides, Rory flew me out so I could take care of the horses. I didn't want anything to eat them."

"Who's Rory?" Lukas asked.

"The steely-blue dragon. He's the one who fought off the dragon that tried to kill us on the way here," she said.

"You can talk to him too?" Frankel asked.

"I guess so."

"Can you talk to them all?" Lukas asked.

"I don't know. I haven't tried. I told him what I needed, and he agreed to take me as long as I promised to return. We aren't in a position to cross them."

"What opening did you go out?" Lukas said.

"One on top of the dome. It won't help us." She turned to the items in front of her—a coil of rope, flint, two hunting knives, two bedrolls, two waterskins, and some dried meat.

Lukas picked up the waterskin Frankel had filled from the nearby water source. "Where did you get this?"

"I found it here."

"It was probably my grandmother's," Ashton said with a sigh. "Did you find anything else she might have left behind?"

"This canopy was already in place. That's one of the reasons I set up camp here."

"It's not like you needed the shade," Lukas said.

"It makes me feel like I have a little more privacy because they can't see me under here," Frankel explained.

"But they know you're here. Evidently we're 'warm' and they can see us even under cover," Ashton said.

"What does that mean?" Lukas asked.

"Not sure, but Rory could see me under the cover of the trees. The horses too."

"I'm sure that's helpful when hunting," Frankel said.

Lukas's stomach went sour, and he put aside the fruit.

"What else did she leave? Any notes? Any writing?" Ashton asked.

"Nothing like that. I found some clay plates, pieces of fabric—I wouldn't quite call them clothes," Frankel said.

"Grandmother was always taking notes. There has to be something."

"But where would she get writing supplies?" Lukas asked.

Ashton shrugged. "She would have had some with her. I suppose she could have made more." She stood and began a thorough search of the rock wall within the canopy. Her hands pushed and prodded the large stones.

Lukas and Frankel joined her. Lukas was on his hands and knees when he called out. "I found a loose rock." He held it up triumphantly.

Ashton dropped down and reached her hand inside the crevice. "Yes!" she exclaimed. She pulled out a leather-bound book.

The three sat as Ashton started to leaf through it. In between the bound pages, additional sheets of coarse paper were stuck in randomly. The ink on the loose pages was various colors, sometimes blue, purple, and even orange.

"She must have been making her own ink," Frankel said in awe. "I only met your grandmother once in the shop. I was impressed with her then; now I'm totally in awe."

Ashton smiled.

"Start at the beginning," Lukas urged her.

Ashton turned to the first page and read aloud.

My dearest Galileo,

I know you'll be angry when you find out where I've gone, but you'll also understand. I'm keeping this journal, so it feels like you are with me on this journey.

Our research has paid off. I think I know where the dragons are. I don't want to get your hopes up, so I didn't want to say anything until I have proof. I'll be home soon.

My dearest,

The forest at the foothills of the Silent Mountain was dark and sinister, but I don't see why mature adults would fear them. I felt eyes following my trail, but not more so than near our village when the wolves are roaming.

The closer I got to the mountain, the calmer I felt. But nothing prepared me for the sight when I broke free of the dark trees and took in the beauty of the Pern Valley. I can't wait to bring you here.

I thought crossing the bridge would frighten me (you know how I am with heights), but I was able to cross with nothing but joy at the scenery.

Now I'm getting to the most exciting part. Dragons, my darling! Dragons! Alive and well. They soared high above, swooping down as if to greet me. I felt no fear; only the euphoria of gliding and playing. Like when we used to take the horses out for a run and give them their head.

Before I knew it, I stood before the opening to the mountain itself. I expected the darkness of a cave and was surprised to discover a hidden meadow of grasses within.

I found plenty of nourishment here and a lake nearby for bathing. Oh, my Galileo, you will be so amazed at the vibrant colors!

Dear One,
Today I met your queen. She is more beautiful than you could have dreamed. She is everything we discussed and so much more.

"Wait a minute," Frankel interrupted her reading. "Why wasn't she afraid of the dragons? They scared me half to death."

Ashton placed her finger in the book to save her place. "You've met my grandfather. My family has always been staunch supporters and believers. We have a legacy passed down from mother to daughter with teachings about dragons."

"Are you for real right now?" Frankel asked.

Lukas laughed. "You get used to it."

"Honestly, I didn't think much about it until recently. Galileo just passed me the book." She pulled it from an inner pocket of her tunic and showed him before sliding it back in place. "I'm still not sure what it all means."

"Well, somehow your grandmother figured out how to find the dragons. We still don't know if that's a good thing or a bad thing," Lukas said.

"I'm not feeling good about it," Frankel said. "We're prisoners."

"Grandmother felt we needed the dragons for some reason. She wasn't clear in the journal she left, but from the stacks of notes she took, it looks like it has to do with the crops."

"What could dragons have to do with farming?" Lukas asked.

"Maybe they plowed the fields," Frankel said.

Ashton and Lukas gave him a strange look.

He bristled. "Well, it's hard work, and they are pretty massive. They could get it done in no time."

Then Ashton burst out laughing. Lukas couldn't contain his grin. "Can you picture a dragon strapped to a plow? Where would their wings go?" she said.

"They wouldn't need a plow. Have you looked at those talons? They could turn a field with a few passes," Frankel said indignantly.

Ashton wiped her eyes with the back of her hand. "We don't mean to laugh, Frankel. We needed to."

Frankel smiled too. "I guess it would be tough for them to get the seeds out of the bags."

"They could poke holes in the bottom with their claws and let the seeds trickle out," Lukas said, using his hands to demonstrate.

As their laughter died down, Ashton opened to where she had left off. She read aloud about her grandmother's time inside the mountain for what seemed to be about fourteen days. A rumbling from Lukas's stomach made her look up.

"Guess we should take a break." She placed the book where they found it and replaced the stone.

"Not sure who she was hiding this book from, but I don't want to take any chances."

They emerged from under the canopy. While not bright by full-sun standards, the light streaming in from the holes overhead still made them squint until their eyes adjusted.

Frankel walked them through the fields, pointing out edible plants and which ones to avoid. Some were foreign to them, so they passed them by, not willing to risk it. Then they refilled their waterskins and sat down to eat as they watched the dragons on the ledge.

"It's creepy how they always seem to be watching," Frankel said.

"I feel like an animal they're studying," Lukas added. He turned to Ashton. "Did you try talking to any of the others yet?"

"I can try."

The men watched in silence as Ashton focused on sending out her message. She spotted Rory and selected the dragon to his left. She wasn't sure about the proper way to address a dragon when she didn't know its name. After a few attempts and failures on various beasts, she turned her attention to Rory.

"Rory, can you hear me?"

"Yes, of course."

"Why can't the others?"

He turned his massive head to his left and right. "Not all have the gift," he said, looking at her.

"How can I tell?"

"You can't."

His simple declaration was not followed by an explanation.

"Well?" Lukas asked. He couldn't stand the silence any longer.

Ashton shook her head. "Rory said not all dragons have the gift, and I can't tell which do and which don't."

A sudden breeze announced the arrival of Rory on the meadow floor.

"Brindisi will see you now," he said.

Ashton stood.

"Where are you going?" Lukas asked.

"The queen calls."

Both men stood. "Take us with you," Frankel said.

Ashton asked Rory, "Can they come?"

There was a pause. Ashton assumed Rory was communicating with Brindisi.

Moments later, two more dragons flattened the grasses in front of the humans. Ashton demonstrated how to step within the creatures' grasps and hold on.

Chapter 24

Nikolai stood, pulling the belt on his robe tightly. The woman in his bed rolled over and placed a pillow over her ears to block out the men's voices.

Bayard patiently waited for the chancellor to accept the hot drink he offered on a tray.

"What is first for today?" Taking the cup, he looked at the sleeping lump on the mattress with disdain. "Or should I say second?"

"You wanted to see the master scholar, sir. She awaits you downstairs."

"Fetch my clothes."

Bayard nodded and moved to do his bidding.

"What of my nephew? My brother said he expected him back today. Have we heard anything?"

"Nothing, sir. But the men in the foothills have seen no signs of him either. Maybe something afoul has happened."

Nikolai froze as he considered. "Not yet. For now, he's a better heir than that simpleton brother of mine. Until one of these wenches you bring me is with child, I need him alive."

Bayard finished buttoning Nikolai's jacket, then walked to the door. With one loud rap, the doors opened, and the guards stood aside at attention as Nikolai passed to meet with Master Gena.

When he entered the throne room, he found her standing patiently with her hands clasped behind her back, no signs of discomfort at having been left waiting for so long without a seat. He noted her lack of nervousness and that she didn't snap to attention. He'd have to remedy that.

He took his seat without acknowledging her.

"Chancellor, you asked to see me," Master Gena said politely.

He crossed his legs and draped his arms over the side of the throne.

Finally he turned his gaze on her. "What do you know of the dragons?"

"Chancellor?"

"You are the master scholar. You're supposed to be the teacher. So tell me what you know about the beasts Galileo and his ilk go on and on about."

She folded her hands in front of her and spoke in a slow, rhythmic tone. "Legend has it that reptiles of enormous proportion once came from the depths of the Silent Lake and grew wings from what used to be their fins. As the creatures grew larger, they began eating livestock and attacking citizens. It wasn't until the Cabot reign that Olmerta was freed from the oppression."

"Yes, yes." Nikolai made a circular motion with his hands. "I know all of that. Tell me what you learned in the vaults."

She spread her arms, palms up. "We found nothing of interest. We looked through many of the books, but they were boring records."

"I saw your scribbles. Looked like the writing of a juvenile. What was noteworthy?"

Looking at a spot over the chancellor's right shoulder, the master scholar envisioned her notes. "Well, we found some references to eggshells retrieved on the banks of the lake. There were lists of offenses and the reparation paid by the city coffers."

"The damned fools almost bankrupted the city before the Cabots were able to set it to rights," Nikolai muttered.

"The fools?"

Nikolai glared at her. "The advisors to my ancestors. What else?"

"The dragons were oft about Olmerta, then they were gone," Master Gena finished.

"Any trace of why they were gone?"

"I assume they died off. It is the way of certain creatures."

Nikolai sprang to his feet. "Obviously not. They are terrorizing our citizens again. Something must be done."

Master Gena held her tongue.

"Did you find any way to kill the beasts?"

"There was nothing that specific in the vault. As I said, it was droll and insignificant. I'm not sure why the palace bothers with the lock at all."

"That's not your place to question," Nikolai snapped. When he turned away from her, he allowed a small smile to crack his face. *One less thing to worry about if there was nothing to be found.*

But then it dawned on him; why was his uncle so keen to share the secret of the vault with him? He insinuated there was more to the family story than Nikolai's father had communicated to him.

Maybe this scholar wasn't as smart as everyone gave her credit for.

When Master Gena took her leave and was out of sight of the palace, she took in a deep breath and exhaled slowly. Not good enough. She needed to go through the process twice more before she calmed her racing heart.

Of all the inconsiderate, careless . . . Gena started the breathing exercise over again. It wouldn't do to show emotion in this case. She had to stick with the story that there was nothing to be found in the vault.

When she had gone looking for Lukas after his audience with the chancellor, he had already left to hunt for the dragons. She hoped he had enough sense to take care. They had barely scratched the surface of the hidden secrets. She wasn't sure what he would be walking into. Would the dragons greet him or hunt him down in exchange for the treatment his ancestors bestowed on them?

She shuddered at the thought. Many in Olmerta saw Lukas's reign as the only thing that may right the failing village. They had to hang on through Nikolai's tenure and pray for no natural-born heirs. Or maybe do more than pray.

Chapter 25

"A new clutch is being laid," the queen told Ashton without preamble.

"And what am I supposed to do about it?" she said using mind-speak.

Hot steam escaped Brindisi's nose, drawing the men's rapt attention away from the sparkling cavern walls.

"What's going on?" Lukas whispered.

"Eggs are being laid, and she wants our help," Ashton told them.

"Why should we help? We're prisoners," Frankel said.

Ashton directed her attention to the dragon. "Will you release us?"

The queen and Ashton locked eyes, although the *sentsentia* connection was silent for a long moment. Finally, Brindisi nodded her head once.

"What do you want us to do?" Ashton spoke her words out loud for the sake of the men.

"Rosa discovered a way to harden the eggs so they could go to full term. We need you to apply the paste."

"What paste? Where is it?"

"You need to produce it."

"How?"

"Rosa knew."

Ashton waited but nothing else was forthcoming. Frustrated, she stormed toward the tunnel entrance. Startled, the men had to hurry to catch up. At the entrance to the tunnel, Ashton stopped abruptly. Lukas sidestepped at the last moment to avoid running into her, but Frankel's reactions weren't quite so fast. He bumped into her before he could catch himself.

She didn't bother turning around when she spoke to Brindisi silently. "We'll need to go outside to get supplies."

"Rory will take you where you need to go."

Ashton started walking again.

"What was that all about?" Lukas asked when they were safely under the canopy.

Ashton had immediately pulled out Rosa's journals. Now she was leafing through pages quickly, looking for anything resembling a formula. "If we want to go home, we need to help her save the eggs. She said Grandmother made a paste to put on the shells so the eggs would harden. If she did, she would have written it down."

After several moments, Ashton found the page she was looking for. Skimming it, she explained to the others.

"Looks like she ran a lot of experiments. She has formulas listed, then many things crossed out and new things added. My guess is it took a while." Ashton squinted at the page. "There's a note at the bottom that says something's missing. She wasn't sure what but thought it had something to do with the water."

Ashton dropped the book into her lap and stared at nothing.

"I know that look," Lukas said.

"I don't. What does it mean?" Frankel asked.

"She has an idea."

The men waited for her to speak.

"We need to gather some ingredients," she finally said. "Frankel, do you know where this is?" She showed him a picture of a plant in the book with red, feather-like leaves.

"Sure. There are rows of it past the cave's water supply."

"I'll need a lot of it." She turned to Lukas. "Grandmother tried this internal water source for the mixture, but it didn't work. What if we tried the lake water outside?"

"It might be the same source," he replied.

"But it might have different properties in it depending on the surrounding ground and the filtering rocks. It's worth a try. Besides, it'll get us out of here for a while."

Frankel froze. "Are you going to leave me here?"

"Of course not. We need to build up trust a little at a time. We'll keep coming back," she assured him.

"How much water do you need?" Lukas asked.

She referred to the formula again. "A lot. I wonder if it's easier to take the plants to the water or bring the water to the plants."

"I think plants to the water. Paste will be easier to transport than water. It may be heavier, but it won't spill as easily," Lukas said.

"We'll still need something to carry it in."

Frankel left to harvest the plants, while Ashton and Lukas expanded their search around the camp in widening circles.

"Rosa had to have something she mixed it in," Lukas said.

Ashton looked up to find Rory watching them. "Do you know what my grandmother used to mix the paste?"

"It's in the hatching grounds," he said.

"Can you take it to the lake for me?" she asked.

Without a response, he was gone. Ashton and Lukas joined Frankel. Together, they dragged cut branches from the plant to the middle of the meadow where the dragons could pick them up. Then they walked to the entrance.

A large, rust-colored dragon lounged in front of the opening.

"Rory, we need to get to the water," Ashton spoke in her head. "Can you have the plants we left brought out to us?"

Slowly, the dragon blocking their path moved aside, then settled into inactivity.

Once in the direct sunlight, Frankel stood with his arms held wide and head tilted back. "You don't appreciate the little things until you don't have them anymore."

Ashton smiled at him. "Come on. The lake is this way."

She led them through the trees to the opening where the horses were. They trotted up to the trio as if truly happy to see them. Lukas held his empty hand out to Zephyr. "Sorry, no fruit this time. I'll see what I can do."

While he continued patting down the horses, Ashton searched the tree line for a large stick to stir with.

When she heard a loud splash, she whirled around to find Frankel resurfacing in the lake. "It feels so good to bathe!" he yelled before diving under again.

Ashton laughed and resumed her search. Selecting a few candidates, she tapped them hard on the ground. The one that didn't break, she deemed strong enough to stir the paste. She picked up a few wider, shorter pieces to serve as scoops. She had no idea how big the eggs would be or how much paste she needed, but her grandmother's recipe seemed to make a large batch.

By the time she returned to where Rory had dropped the crude tub made from a tree stump, Lukas had collected large stones. "We can use these to grind up the plants," he said.

Frankel wrung out his outer clothes and laid them on a rock to dry before joining them

They set to work, Ashton giving directions. First, she had Rory pick up the tub and fill it with water. By the time he placed it near their workspace, a third of the water had sloshed out, soaking Lukas in the process.

Lukas spluttered. "He did that on purpose!"

Ashton laughed, handing him a rock. "Start grinding."

They worked diligently, Ashton estimating measurements from her grandmother's notes. She stirred the contents, using the scoops to test the consistency. When she thought it was close, she wiped her hands on her tunic. "Do we have time for a dip before heading in?"

"Ask your friend." Lukas tilted his head toward Rory.

A moment later, Ashton said, "We have a little time before the eggs are laid." She kicked off her boots and started stripping off her clothes as she walked into the water.

150

Frankel took advantage of another chance to swim. Lukas hung back, watching as Ashton peeled off her undershirt and submerged herself in the lake.

"Come on," she called to him. "It may be a long time in between baths, and our clothes already have days of dirt on them."

Lukas sat on a nearby rock to remove his boots. He averted his eyes as Ashton emerged from the water to wring out her clothes and lay them next to Frankel's.

"You're taking forever," she chided him as she ran to the lake in nothing but her clingy underclothes.

He waited until she turned her back to remove the last of his outer garments. Carrying them in front of him, he walked into the water up to his waist and focused on scrubbing out the dirt.

Frankel and Ashton were now swimming near the center of the lake. Lukas dashed for the rock to drape his clothes, then quickly made it to the safety of the water.

After a while of playing and splashing like little kids, Ashton headed for the shore. "Rory says it's time."

"Time for what?" Frankel asked.

"The laying of the clutch."

They followed her to where their clothes were now nicely dry and warm. They dressed quickly, their backs to each other for some semblance of privacy.

When they were finished, Rory returned to carry the tub and paste to the hatching grounds. "Hurry," he told Ashton.

The trio jogged through the wooded path to the opening at the base of the mountain. When they arrived, three dragons awaited them. Ashton approached one and allowed herself to be scooped up. The men followed her lead. In no time, they were lifted above the opening and around the mountain, approaching from the opposite direction.

When they were deposited on the high ledge, it took them a minute to regain their balance and walk straight.

"I won't ever get used to flying," Frankel said.

"Sure beats walking," Lukas commented.

"This way." Ashton ducked into a dark tunnel, following it through twists and turns until it opened into a chamber. Unlike the sparkling cave where Brindisi stayed, this cave wasn't as bright. Sand covered the floor, and there was nothing colorful.

"Kind of dreary for a birthing room, isn't it?" Frankel said.

A roar followed by a burst of heat hit them. They raised their arms to shield their faces.

"Some things seem to be similar between humans and dragons," Ashton commented. "It doesn't sound like a painless process."

The wooden tub was where Rory had placed it near the laboring beast. "Rory says she's done."

"Is it safe to get close?" Lukas asked.

"Just move slowly." Using *sentsentia*, Ashton reached out to the mother to calm her and let her know they were trying to help.

The huge head swung around to look at them, but she moved slightly, giving them room to approach.

Frankel reached the eggs first. "I count seven." He touched one. "They're pretty soft and a little slimy." He wiped his hand on his pants.

Lukas and Ashton grabbed scoops from inside the barrel and carefully carried the paste to the egg. Working together, they covered all seven eggs with a thick coat of paste. When they finished, Ashton went to the first egg. "It's hardening. I wonder if we should roll them to get the underside."

Lukas pushed on the egg. "I won't be easy."

Ashton told the mother what they were trying to do. With the tip of her nose, she nudged one egg, then the others, until their soft side was exposed. Frankel and Lukas went for more paste.

"Now what?" Frankel asked when they had finished.

Ashton wiped her hands on the rough wall. Although the paste dried quickly on the eggs, on her hands, it was still as soft as when they started. She checked the contents of the wooden vat. "Not much left. I hope they don't need a second coat."

"What did your grandmother have to say about it?" Lukas said.

Ashton sat in the sand with her back to the wall. Turning to the formula page in the journal, she scanned for the answer. "She tried a second and even a third coat, but it seems the eggs didn't usually make it. She even tried different things for the same clutch." Ashton went silent as she read to herself. She summarized for her friends.

"The father wasn't very happy about the experiment, but Brindisi understood the need. With that clutch, she tried various coats. Once she got past three, the baby dragon couldn't break out. One wasn't enough. Two is the best bet, even though the dragons came out scrawny. Some didn't live more than a few days."

"I can't imagine a scrawny dragon," Frankel said.

She stood. "We need to make more. Do you think we have enough plants?"

"Plenty. Let's go before it gets dark," Frankel said.

Chapter 26

After eight days of keeping an around-the-clock vigil, the three friends fell, exhausted, into their beds of pine boughs. When she closed her eyes, the pale dragon-like forms that had emerged from five of the seven eggs haunted Ashton's dreams. Two of the eggs had never hatched.

Frankel had tried singing to them, as he had done with his son when he was little. Still, when the eggs finally hatched, the almost translucent skin stretched over the delicate bones was heartbreaking. One at a time, the mother had picked up each baby and flown out through the single opening in the dome. She always came back alone.

When she didn't return after the fifth flight, Lukas had picked up a stone to break one of the remaining eggs. With the appearance of the first crack, something oozed from underneath the shell, dampening the sand around it. Lukas jumped as if burnt.

The smell in the cave was too much to bear, and they had made their way to the rock ledge.

Now, as she wished for sleep without dreams, the overwhelming sadness eventually pulled her into a restless slumber.

The next morning, Lukas awoke to find Ashton busy scribbling on some of the loose pages she had sewn together using plant fiber and bone fragments.

He handed her a waterskin. "Any ideas?"

"Grandmother was sure it was the right plant. She tried many different combinations over the years before landing on this one. The only other variable was water."

"What about the cave itself?"

"What do you mean?"

"This may be nothing," Lukas said, "but in some of those old records Master Gena and I found, they took a lot of time cataloging eggshells."

Ashton looked up in surprise. "What about the eggshells?"

Lukas took the waterskin and took a long drink. "They were very interested in tracking dragon eggshells they found on the beach of the Silent Lake. There were pages of how many they found and where they moved them to."

"They moved them?" Ashton asked.

He nodded. "Most of the time to a farmer's field. No names I recognized."

Ashton got excited. "If dragon eggshells were found near the lake, maybe that's the water source that we need. Did they say shells or eggs? Specifically?"

Lukas thought about it. "It was shells. They talked about how many pieces the shells cracked into, and how they were divided up."

"Silent Lake might be the answer. And it makes sense. The water supply is from this mountain."

"So if we need that water, how are we going to get it? There's no way the queen is going to let us go that far."

"Even if she did, the villagers wouldn't be too keen to see the dragons on the shore," Frankel said, plopping down beside Ashton. They hadn't even heard him approach.

"We'll cross that bridge when we come to it," she said. "For now, let's figure out how we're going to convince Brindisi this is what's good for her wing."

"But why not?" Ashton sat on a high rock inside the crystal cavern. From the evidence of dried pine boughs, she suspected her grandmother had also taken advantage of the height to get on a more even keel with the much taller dragon. "Lukas says records of dragon eggs on the beaches of Silent Lake exist. That means you were there at one time."

"That was before," the queen said.

"Before what?"

"Before the humans of Olmerta decided to withdraw from our agreement."

"I don't understand."

Ashton was sure the queen rolled her eyes. The golden crystals appeared more frightening than if they were on a human. She continued speaking in her slow manner.

"Humans are greedy creatures. They want everything immediately and easily. They do not have patience or good sense, expecting us to labor *for* them as if their time was superior to ours."

"So what happened?"

"We refused. In return, they fired at us with projectiles. If it were not for your family line, I would have rid all of Olmerta of humans."

"What does my family line have to do with it?"

"Members of your clan came to us—at great risk—offering healing. They removed the sharp bits embedded into the soft hide not covered by scales, administering salve to speed the healing process. Not all were saved."

Ashton was shocked. She had never heard this part of the story. How could humans turn on such lovely creatures? Especially if they had worked together for so long. Why the change?

As if hearing her thoughts—and perhaps she *had* heard them—Brindisi answered. "I lost communication with Queen Ashlea and felt an emptiness like never before."

As the wave of desolation hit Ashton, a rush of sympathy flowed out. She felt her awareness, warm and fluid, wrap around something she recognized as Brindisi. It was oddly comforting.

The queen's countenance relaxed perceptibly. "After that, things did not return to as they once were."

When Ashton gathered her thoughts, she asked, "Who is Queen Ashlea?"

"Child, how can you ask me this? Why do you not know yourself?"

"We haven't had a queen in my lifetime or my grandfather's. No one talks of queens. Lukas saw a picture in a book, but he wasn't sure if it was real."

"Queen Ashlea was a gentle soul. As was her mother before her and even her mother before." Brindisi paused, and Ashton sensed her searching for something. "We feared something was amiss because

157

Queen Ashlea had less and less time to spend with us. She did not speak directly of her difficulties, but I felt she was saddened and frightened by something going on in the village."

"What would frighten a queen?"

Brindisi harrumphed at this, and Ashton felt it in her chest. "Sadly, many things can frighten queens, especially if they threaten to harm her wing."

The large dragon shifted her position and crossed her front legs. "Discontent spreads from many corners—young ones who grow without knowing where they came from or the reason for the way of things."

"Do you have these problems with your wing?" Ashton wasn't sure if it was a rude question, but the thought passed to the dragon before she had a chance to sensor it.

Brindisi's slow speech seemed to emphasize her concern. "More so lately. As our clutches are becoming smaller and our hatchlings are weaker, some of the younger members think they can do better on their own. It is important to regain our strength and unite my dragons."

"Will you let us at least try? When is your next clutch due?"

"Within the next three moon sets."

"Why not try the Silent Lake?

Brindisi shook her massive head. "What is to guarantee the safety of my wing?"

"Lukas is the chancellor's nephew. He can provide protection."

Brindisi hissed and flames came from her nostrils. "This Lukas, what is his family name?"

"Cabot. He's the head of the soldiers."

Brindisi was up on four legs with such speed that Ashton took several startled steps backward. "What's wrong?"

"The Cabots are not to be trusted. They gave Queen Ashlea dark moods."

"It's true that Chancellor Nikolai isn't a pleasant person, but Lukas is much different than his uncle. He's been helping with the eggs."

"The Cabot boy stays here. If he is truly the leader of the soldiers, they will not risk harm to him."

"But that's ridiculous," Ashton said. "Lukas hasn't done anything to you. Why would you threaten him?"

"If the humans do not threaten my wing, there is no threat to the Cabot boy."

What was Lukas going to say? He wasn't going to be happy about being a hostage. Somehow, she was going to have to regain the trust of Brindisi and her wing if humans and dragons were to live together again.

Ashton wrestled with the idea. She wasn't sure how the villagers were going to react when she told them about the dragons coming back.

"I need to at least take Frankel with me. His family and the people need to know he's safe and that no harm came to him."

Brindisi nodded.

Returning Frankel would help, but there was still the matter of the missing soldiers.

"What about the other soldiers who disappeared? Did you find out anything?"

Brindisi was quiet. "I fear some rogue members of my wing may have had something to do with their disappearance," she admitted haltingly.

Ashton couldn't interpret the feeling she was getting through their bond. "What does that mean?"

"When the humans refused to communicate, some members of my wing blamed it on arrogance."

Ashton was incredulous. "So they killed them?"

"I fear that is a likely scenario. Whether it was intentional or accidental, I cannot say. No one can truly say. It could be that the humans lashed out, and my wing defended themselves."

"If they lashed out, it's only because you took them from their post in Olmerta. What did you expect?"

"What is done is done," Brindisi said. "What we do next is between us."

Ashton wasn't sure how she felt about this. She was sure Lukas would not be happy when he heard about the soldiers. She probably shouldn't tell him. At least not yet.

"When you get back, go to Lieutenant Raquel first," Lukas told her.

"First, I'm going to see my grandfather."

"Okay, after your grandfather. Find Lieutenant Raquel. Give her this." He handed her the scroll he had been working on since Ashton had relayed the conditions from Brindisi.

"She can set up a perimeter and make it inconspicuous. We don't want to arouse the suspicion of the townspeople. And we *certainly* don't want the chancellor to find out. Then find Master Gena. Tell her what we've learned. She'll know what to do."

Lukas smacked a tree. "I hate that I'm not the one going."

Frankel put a hand on his shoulder. "I'll take good care of her."

"I don't need anybody to take care of me," Ashton said.

Lukas turned red. "I meant it would be easier for me to set the perimeter. I know that area."

"Raquel is very capable. She'll be able to handle it," Frankel reassured him.

Chapter 27

Master Gena sorted through the papers on her desk, frantically searching for her notes. She had written down as much as she could remember after the personal guard had removed her and Lukas from the vault. Her memory was solid, so she supposed she captured all the relevant points.

Ah-ha! Gena spread the pages on the desk next to the notes she had taken during her conversation with Ashton. She was relieved to hear Lukas was safe—at least for now. But they had to ensure the hatching went well to bring him home. And then what?

She wasn't sure, but she was determined to figure it out.

She poured through the notes again, trying to apply the information Ashton had shared with her to what she found in the old records.

As a scholar, Gena was overjoyed at the idea of bringing dragons into Olmerta. In her circles, dragons were highly thought of, even though they were rarely discussed, due to the Cabot lineage's disapproval of such subjects. Any mention of dragons had been stricken from the official records and educational tomes for many an age now.

But no worthy scholar could truly erase anything historical. Dragon lore was passed mouth to mouth and with cryptic notes from master scholar to master scholar. Now Gena had new information to add to the records, and she was elated.

Ashton's suggestion that the dragon's hatching ground was on the sands near Silent Lake rang true to everything Gena pieced together. Eggshells were picked up from the beaches and distributed to villagers. There was no mention of why, but it was important enough to write down and ensure equity amongst the families.

As she looked over the table she had recreated from memory, a thought came to her. *What do these families have in common?* She went to a bookshelf in her study and searched the highest reaches, pulling down a heavy volume not often referenced.

Flipping through the pages, she looked for similar names. She knew the tomes from the vault were approximately three hundred generations old, so she started there.

Scratching notes furiously on parchment, she went from volume to volume, until she reached present-day records of genealogy. Names had changed through marriage, and then sometimes even changed back generations later.

Her stomach growled. She had been at this for hours, but she thrived on research. It would have to be enough to sustain her a little longer.

When she looked at the final list of names in front of her, she checked it twice to make sure she wasn't missing something. She knew most of these families—had taught many of the children and even some of the parents herself. There *was* a common thread. Farmers. These families were farmers.

Although land switched hands occasionally due to deaths or debt, it was most common for property to remain in a family for many generations.

She sat on her stool, staring into the distance. *Why would farmers need eggshells?*

A knock on her door broke her train of thought.

Three days later, Ashton and Galileo sat on the still-warm sand in a secluded area next to Silent Lake. The second sun had set, and a full moon reflected off the water, giving them plenty of light to see by.

The woods were unusually quiet. Ashton supposed it was the presence of Lieutenant Raquel's soldiers amongst the trees that scared off the wildlife.

Soon, a shadow passed in front of the night light, and Ashton recognized the shape. "He's here."

"That's going to be hard to get used to," Galileo said.

"What is?" Ashton rose to greet the heavy-laden dragon.

Galileo stood as well. "Fathers bearing the young. I was there when your mother was born. I wouldn't have traded places with your grandmother for the world."

Ashton laughed. "No, I don't suppose you would have."

A large dragon with green scales tipped in gold landed effortlessly in the sand.

Ashton reached out with her *sentsentia.* "Welcome, Cyprus."

A warm stroke reached across her mind, then a sharp stab of pain.

Ashton winced. Galileo grabbed her arm. "What is it? What's wrong."

The pain was gone as quickly as it appeared. "I'm fine."

Then an apologetic voice in her head said, "I'm sorry. I didn't know that would happen. Rosa wasn't around for my last clutch."

"You knew my grandmother?"

"She was a powerful human, much beloved."

For the sake of Galileo, she spoke out loud. "This is my grandfather Galileo. He was Rosa's mate."

"Many thanks to you, Grandfather, for sharing your Rosa with us."

Galileo's eyes went wide. "Did he—? Did I—?"

Ashton laughed again. Then abruptly the connection was broken. It was like being dumped in cold water.

"Cyprus? Cyprus? Are you okay?"

A moment later, Cyprus returned to her mentally. "I'm here. Trust me. You didn't want to experience that with me. It's time."

Ashton pointed to a hole dug in the sand. She and Galileo had lined the bottom with the red, feathery plant from the mountain. "It would be easiest if you could lay your eggs in there. Is that possible?"

Cyprus lumbered over to the hole. "A little privacy at this point would be appreciated," he said.

Ashton and Galileo walked to the trees. When they were within a few steps, Raquel joined them. "She's beautiful!"

"She's a he," Ashton said.

"What? How's that even possible?"

"If you haven't noticed, they aren't built like us. Who knows what's possible?"

Raquel shook her head. "I wouldn't have believed it if I didn't see it with my own eyes. I thought you were crazy when you fed me this story. I only went

along with it because Lukas would kill me if I didn't."
She glanced again at the beast. "I'm sure glad I did."

It was another hour before Ashton felt the tired
but pleased sense brush her mind. "You may come
close now."

Ashton gestured for the others to follow. In the
hole lay four mottled gray eggs.

"We're going to cover them. Galileo, get the
buckets ready."

As Ashton and Raquel shoveled sand over the
eggs, Galileo dumped bucket after bucket into the
hole.

Cyprus rested nearby.

"Now what?" Raquel asked.

Ashton stuck her shovel in the sand. "We wait."

Chapter 28

Five days passed before the sand started to stir. Galileo felt it first and shook Ashton awake. It was deep night, and she was still groggy until she heard Cyprus calling to her. "I'm coming."

They had decided it was best for Cyprus to stay away during the day when there was a chance anyone might stumble upon the beach. More people had heard the story of the dragon taking Frankel, therefore, there were more believers now who may be able to see them.

As a precaution, Frankel had agreed to return to his family to ease their suffering but remain missing to everyone else so as not to arouse too much curiosity. It would be hard to explain where he was without mentioning dragons. He would be able to venture out again after this experiment. For now, he was content to be home.

Cyprus must have heard his dragonettes calling to him as he landed nearby seconds later. Ashton watched the great beast gently digging away the sand with great haste.

Galileo, Ashton, and Cyprus investigated the four dark blue, rocking eggs in the pit. Ashton felt the wave of pride coming from Cyprus as he looked on.

The two humans turned toward the sound of running feet. Raquel slid to a stop in front of them, breathless. "I sent for Master Gena as soon as I felt it. Did I miss anything?"

She gazed into the pit and an expression of wonder crossed her face.

A crack was beginning on one of the eggs. Then another. The eggs rocked more violently as the dragonettes fought for release from captivity. Finally, a red snout covered in slimy goo emerged from an opening. As the egg split apart, the crimson baby tumbled out, sand sticking to the slime on its leathery skin.

As it attempted to climb from the hole, Cyprus scooped it up and placed it on the level ground. The newborn waddled its way toward the lake as another egg cracked open, revealing another dragonette with a pinkish covering. One by one, as the dragonettes appeared, they were scooped out by their father, and each made its way to the water where they splashed around in the shallows. When the sand and slime were washed away, the four swam into deeper water, ducking under and coming up with fish in their mouths.

"Oh, my." It was Master Gena. In their enthralled state, they hadn't noticed her arrival.

Ashton greeted her with a huge grin. "Isn't it wonderful?"

"Wonderful, indeed," the master mumbled.

Cyprus had joined his babies in the water, cooing over them as they fed. Before long, he reached out to Ashton. "They've had their fill. We are returning to the mountain. Thank you for your help. I will report the success to the queen."

"Of course. Good luck!"

Cyprus took to the sky. Four smaller smudges of dark against the now-lightening sky rose behind him. The humans stood on the sand watching until they couldn't see the dragons anymore.

"Well, that was a very special treat. Now we need to get these shells moved to my workshop before its full light." Master Gena was intently sketching out the eggs, their placement, and color on a parchment she withdrew from her robe.

Lieutenant Raquel whistled, and troops appeared from the forests, three wagons drawn along behind. Without question, they carefully took the eggshells Master Gena passed out from the hole. Occasionally, she stopped to take a note before resuming her work.

Ashton and Galileo watched but didn't interfere with the process. When the shells were all in the carts with a tarp covering them, the soldiers disappeared into the woods, heading toward the master's cottage.

Galileo and Ashton set to work filling the hole. As they made their way to the path through the trees, they brushed away signs of the wagon tracks in the sand.

Chapter 29

When she heard a knock, Ashton opened the door to her grandfather's cottage cautiously. Seeing Lukas outside, she flung herself into his arms. Caught off guard, he staggered before he wrapped his arms around her and held her tight.

"I'm so glad you're okay," Ashton said. She held on to him a moment longer before stepping back and releasing him.

Galileo joined them at the door and pumped Lukas's hand. "My boy, my boy, it's good to see you in one piece. Thank you for all you've done. For the dragons and Olmerta."

Lukas was touched by the warm welcome.

"Come in and sit." Ashton brought him something to drink and cut him a large wedge of pie. "How did you get here already?"

"I got a ride from our friends. It's much faster than walking."

"I was heading out in the morning to get you." Ashton gestured toward her packed bed roll and food supplies she had laid out. "Zephyr's in the barn. She was very gentle with Frankel, although she did seem upset about leaving you behind."

"She was probably more relieved to be away from the dragons," Lukas said.

"They escorted us out of the foothills. Not sure where they thought we were going to run off to. They had to know we wouldn't take a chance with you still in the mountain."

"I'm glad we saved you the trip," Lukas said, digging into the pie. "They dropped me near the lake, and I walked from there."

"I'm glad Brindisi was good to her word," Ashton said.

"So now what happens?" Galileo asked. "That can't be the end of it. How are we going to get the townspeople to be okay with the dragons returning?"

Lukas put down his fork. "I have to talk to the chancellor. It has to start with him."

Galileo was shaking his head. "That's not a good idea. The way Nikolai has been ranting about the evils of the dragons, I can't imagine he's going to change his mind easily."

"But I have to try. I've taken an oath to serve the city."

Ashton sank into a chair beside him. "Maybe if the people supported the dragons' return, then Nikolai would ease up a bit."

"I can talk to the villagers," Galileo said. "We can get them to understand."

"How's Frankel doing?" Lukas asked.

"He's still in hiding with his family, but now that you're home, he'll be relieved to be able to show his face again."

"Have you seen my mother?" Lukas asked.

Ashton gave a small smile. "I did stop by to reassure her you were okay and would be home soon. But I didn't give her any details, no matter how hard she tried to bribe me with honey-cinnamon biscuits."

"Hmm, those sound good. I'm looking forward to my mother's cooking. Even my father's."

They all chuckled at that.

"Well, I should go present myself and let my parents lecture me about running off." Lukas stood.

Before he walked out the door, Ashton wrapped her arms around his neck again, giving him a tight squeeze and a kiss on the cheek. "I'm so glad you're back," she said.

The next morning, Lukas presented himself to his uncle, smartly dressed and polished. Nikolai rose in surprise as his nephew entered. "Where have you been?" he bellowed.

"It's a long story, sir," Lukas replied.

Nikolai summoned Lukas to approach.

Lukas stood, not quite at attention but certainly not relaxed in front of his uncle.

"I take it you didn't find the dragons you were looking for," Nikolai said.

"Actually, I did."

Nikolai's eyebrows shot up. "So you're here to present me with a head?" He sat down on his throne with exaggerated care.

"No, sir. I've discovered they're much different than we expected. And I am not convinced they are bad for Olmerta."

"Tell that to the tailor who lost his shop or your soldiers' families!"

Lukas stood straighter. "I believe the fire was an unfortunate accident. We still haven't uncovered what happened to the soldiers."

"I take it this means you haven't talked to your lieutenant lately. She has some cockamamie idea about how they left their posts in pursuit of bandits trying to attack the palace."

"No, sir. I came here first."

"You obviously had time to bathe and change. I assume this means you presented yourself to your father before your chancellor."

Lukas gave a slight, apologetic bow. "I didn't want to appear before you disheveled," he explained.

Nikolai waved away his excuse. "What is it you think you know about these creatures?"

"I've seen the queen. All she wants is to live in peace."

"That's what all enemies say as they try to get inside our walls."

"No, they aren't looking for anything from Olmerta. They only want unhindered access to the Silent Lake."

"The dragons surely have other water sources. Why would they need our lake?

"I don't know all the details," Lukas hedged, "but that's their request."

"And how did they pass on this request to you?"

Lukas wasn't sure how to reply. He didn't want to give away the fact that Ashton could speak with the dragons, but he didn't know how else to explain what he had learned.

He gave in. "They can communicate with humans."

Nikolai's eyes widened, and his head bobbed back and forth on his neck like Lukas had seen chickens do. "Then why didn't this queen speak with me, as one ruler to another?"

Lukas cleared his throat. "Not all humans have this gift. Only some can hear them."

"And I suppose you are one of the lucky few," his uncle said. Without giving him time to reply, Nikolai went on. "And they want nothing else. What will they give us in return?"

"What could they possibly have that we need?"

"There's always something."

"We can get them to agree to stay away from our villagers and the livestock."

Nikolai stood. "I will allow them temporary access to Silent Lake only. But if they further harass any of my citizens, they will feel my wrath. Understood?"

Lukas saluted before departing to find out what had been going on while he was in the mountain.

"I got your message," Ashton said, emerging from the cover of the willow tree when Lukas arrived. "What's up?"

"Sorry. I didn't mean to sound so cryptic. It's been hard to get away. I think my uncle's having me followed."

Ashton looked over his shoulder, searching the trees.

"Not this time. I came in a very round-about way to get here. No one is following me."

She relaxed and took his hands in hers. "I'm worried about you. You look horrible."

He squeezed her hands and then dropped them to begin pacing. "While I was gone, Raquel suggested to my uncle that my missing soldiers were lured away from their posts chasing thieves who were trying to get into the palace. That's why there's no trace of foul play."

"Could she be right?" Ashton couldn't look at him as she asked the question.

Lukas stooped to pick up a rock and threw it into the lake. "I suppose. But with what we know, that's not the likely scenario."

"But could they have seen the dragons and gone after them?"

"If that was the case, why didn't they come back? Why haven't we seen any signs of them?" He threw another rock.

Ashton felt the war inside of her as she considered whether or not to tell Lukas about her discussion with Brindisi. She didn't want him to turn on the dragons when they were so close to coming to peaceful terms. "So what are you doing about it?"

"We've sent people into the neighboring villages, inquiring about the missing soldiers or any like happenings in their towns. We don't expect to hear anything for a few days."

He turned to look at her. "Have you heard from Brindisi lately? How are the dragonettes?"

She shook her head. "We can't connect from this distance. I come down to the lake a few times a day in case Rory flies over."

"How's Galileo?"

She smiled. "He's excited. Business at the shop has been slow since Frankel's disappearance, but Grandfather is keeping busy creating new art to fill his shelves."

"I'll bet these new pieces involve dragon eggs."

"Definitely!"

"Now that Nikolai has agreed to give dragons access to the lake, Galileo's business will probably pick up," Lukas said.

"I still can't believe he gave in that easily. He's up to something. Why else would he have you followed?"

A dark shadow briefly blocked the sun. Both Ashton and Lukas searched the sky for wings.

"Our queen sends her regards," Rory spoke into Ashton's head.

Ashton spoke her words so Lukas could be part of the conversation as she answered, "And our regards to her as well. How are the dragonettes?"

"Fine and healthy, thanks to you. Another hatching is due soon. We suspect tomorrow night."

"Tomorrow night? We'll be ready."

Without another word, Rory flew off. Ashton looked at Lukas. "Are you going to tell your uncle?"

He shook his head. "That wasn't a requirement, and I don't see any reason to draw any more attention to the dragons than need be. At least for now."

She agreed. "I'll let Master Gena know. She's awfully excited about the eggshells for some reason."

Chapter 30

The master scholar stood in the garden plot behind her cottage. She couldn't believe what she was seeing. Only a week had past, and already, half her plants were twice as high as the others.

She pulled out her sketch pad and jotted down measurements of each variety. The results were astonishing. Compared to the plants left untreated, those she fertilized with the crushed eggshells were outperforming in every way. Even the vegetables produced were larger by comparison, and the leaves were darker green.

An idea popped into her head, and she ran to her lab to check her theory.

Comparing the crop yield from her earliest records to those currently reported, Gena noted a sharp decline. *Was there a correlation between when the dragons stopped hatching near Silent Lake and the farm production?* she thought.

She needed to get into the vault again. She remembered the names involved, but she couldn't be sure of the tables that listed rows and rows of numbers. Nothing in her library spoke of dragons, so she couldn't be sure of the timing.

She was excited to get to Ashton and find out when the next hatching would be. She needed to run a larger test and needed more shells to do it.

Packing her notes into a leather pouch, she tucked them into a hidden compartment under a floorboard in her sleeping chamber next to a larger, wrapped package. *No sense taking chances.*

Grabbing her walking stick, she rushed out her front door and ran into Ashton.

Ashton stumbled but kept her feet as the scholar apologized profusely.

"How fortuitous!" Gena said. "I was coming to see you."

"There's going to be another hatching," Ashton said.

"So, you've heard from the queen?" Gena asked.

"Rory told me. He said tomorrow night."

"The timing couldn't be better. I'll ready the wagons. Will we have help again?"

"Lukas said he would have Raquel station the guards again to keep away anyone who might wander in accidentally. I'm sure they wouldn't mind bringing the wagons when it's time for the hatching."

Gena clapped her hands together.

The pit had been dug, and the woods were quiet as Galileo, Ashton, and Lukas waited for the arrival of the expectant dragon.

A rush of warm wind caught Ashton's attention, then she saw the yellow dragon gliding in from over the trees. The creature's wings extended as she came in for a graceful landing near the pit.

Ashton stepped forward to greet her just as a dark liquid spouted from the mother's throat around the protruding arrow. She whipped her head back and her wings forward to protect her swollen belly, knocking Ashton to the ground in the process.

A cry rang out as people flooded from the tree line. Ashton crawled to where her grandfather had fallen in the sand. She tried to pull him to his feet as the great beast shot flames at the onslaught.

Another blow hit the yellow creature's wing as she haltingly took to the sky. Her escape was a narrow one, aided by the soldiers who arrived to fight the people waving bows and flinging rocks.

Lukas bellowed orders, and the soldiers captured and downed the renegades. Ashton dragged Galileo to the safety of the pit.

When the fighting ended, the soldiers surrounded a group of twelve dressed in all black. Some were unconscious, and Ashton suspected a few might even be dead. The others were on their knees.

"What the hell!" Lukas screamed in the face of one of the captives.

The woman stayed silent, not at all phased by the bloodshed.

"What's the meaning of this?" he barked.

No one answered.

"Who sent you? Why did you attack?"

Someone snickered. Lukas turned on him. "You think it's funny taking a life?"

"You're one to talk. You're fine with those beasts taking your soldiers."

Lukas backhanded the man, and he fell.

Raquel stepped in, guiding Lukas away from the circle. "I apologize, sir. I don't know what happened."

In the dim light, Lukas read the faces of the soldiers on the beach. All but one stared with hate at the prisoners. That one inspected the lapping water.

"Take this trash to the cells. Bring me Hanson."

Raquel gave him a questioning look but moved out. "Hanson! To the captain. The rest, take your charges and follow the sergeant."

Ashton had pulled herself from the pit and was next to Lukas. "What happened?"

"I suspect Hanson can tell us, can't you?" He directed this question at the soldier standing at attention in front of him.

Hanson said nothing, though his face was pale even in this light.

"What do you have to say for yourself?"

"Sir, I don't know what you—"

"Don't give me that. It's all over your face. Why would you turn on your own?"

"Those monsters are not my own!" he spat. "They took our brothers and sisters, and you side with them! What kind of leader are you?"

Lukas inhaled sharply, then exhaled slowly as he calmed his emotions. Finally, he trusted himself to speak. "Did you see that yellow dragon take our soldiers and didn't come forward?"

Hanson started. "No, of course I didn't withhold information—"

"Then how are you so sure this dragon took our people?" Lukas spoke loudly, with an edge to his voice.

The soldier had the good sense to look contrite, and he lowered his gaze.

"Show me the evidence!" Lukas was in his face now, forcing the man to look up.

Hanson had no words.

"You disgust me. Remove that tunic and join your partners in the cells." Lukas waved a hand, and Raquel stepped forward, grasping the man by the upper arm. Hanson went along without resisting.

When they were gone, Lukas ran a hand over his weary face. "How bad is it when I can't trust my soldiers?"

Ashton stroked his arm as she spoke. "They're human too. Who knows who's filling their heads with ideas? You can't expect them not to have opinions."

"I expect them to follow orders!" Lukas snapped.

Ashton knew he needed time and space to process this betrayal. *Betrayal!* She needed to get to Brindisi!

"I have to go. Get Grandfather home, please."

"Where are you going?" Lukas asked.

"I have to talk to Brindisi. I have to convince her this wasn't us." Ashton ran off into the trees, rushing home to get Sheba.

Chapter 31

Sheba was foaming at the mouth as Ashton pushed her to a faster pace.

"I'm sorry, girl," she yelled into her ear. "It's a matter of life or death."

As they reached the foothills, Ashton was assaulted by cries of pain, fear, and anger. She had to focus to stay in the saddle.

Seeing Rory's blue scales hovering near the yellow dragon on the ground, Ashton pulled Sheba up short and slid off. She ran to the dragon's side.

The large yellow head flashed toward her, stopping her in her tracks. "Rory, tell her . . . it wasn't us. I swear!"

Rory rocked while the yellow beast placed her head on her front legs, guarding the piece of wood extending two feet from her throat.

"Let me check her neck. I brought supplies." Ashton pulled off her pack and approached the dragon with her arms outstretched.

Rory spoke. "Quickly. She's lost a lot of blood."

Ashton's hands ran over the dragon's neck. The spear had gone through her throat and was jutting from the back of her neck where the point had dislodged one of her scales.

"I have to get it out so I can stop the bleeding," Ashton told her and Rory at the same time. "The end of the spear has a barb on it, so I can't pull it out without causing more damage. I need to push it through."

Ashton felt the grunt of agreement in her head. She laid out the supplies she would need to patch the wound once the spear was out, so they were within easy reach.

"Rory, can you help me with this part? I'll push on this end. As soon as you can, grab the spear and pull. Make sure to pull straight out. Can you do that? Can you get a hold of the tip?"

Rory positioned his pointed snout over his kinsman. "I'm ready."

Ashton projected calm feelings and visions of the crystal cavern in the mountain into the mother's head at the same time as trying to mask her own emotions and fear.

She stepped closer, and the dragon raised her head to give Ashton access to the stick. Ashton took hold, and without giving the dragon time to reconsider, she shoved upward with as much force as she could muster. After the wider point of the spear broke free of the scales, the shaft moved easily.

Ashton felt it pulled from her hands as Rory grasped the other end. She rushed to her supplies and quickly packed the hole with bags of healing herbs and clotting material. When she finished with the front, she bade the mother to rest her head so Ashton could reach the back of her neck. She quickly packed that hole as well, and the bleeding stopped.

She wiped her bloody hands on the grass and went to check on Sheba.

The horse was panting. As Ashton approached, Sheba stumbled as she stepped away. Her head jerked from side to side as if she were looking for something.

A spear struck the ground at her feet. Sheba reared up, colliding with Ashton as she landed. The force knocked Ashton over, saving her from another arrow that embedded itself in Sheba's saddlebag. The horse ran toward home. Ashton didn't blame her.

She looked around, trying to spy her attackers. Rory was spraying fire, and human screams reached her ears as the blaze caught hold. Four flaming, man-shaped objects materialized from the forest. They took several steps in her direction before falling on what was left of their burnt faces. The grasses around their bodies sizzled and steamed, thankfully not catching fire as well.

The screaming stopped, and it was quiet in the field again.

When she turned, Rory was staring at the lump of cloudy gray ovals laying in the grass. Ashton rushed to the mother. "I don't have any paste. I don't know what to do."

The yellow head swiveled away, and Ashton felt the unbearable sadness. Then the beast got to her feet, took a few steps, and launched herself clumsily into the sky. She barely cleared the trees, then she was gone.

Ashton wiped tears away with the back of her hand. The smell of iron and grass assaulted her nostrils. She turned to the eggs. "Maybe we can transport them to the beach," she told Rory. "Can you carry them?"

"It's too late. They're gone."

"We can't leave them here. Let's at least bury them."

"Step back," Rory said.

Ashton retreated, and Rory shot a directed flare, incinerating the eggs in a flash.

Suddenly, Ashton was driven to her knees as a searing pain cut through her mourning.

"I should never have trusted you!" the voice of the queen cried.

Ashton cradled her head, trying to protect herself but not knowing where to start. "We didn't . . . I mean, it wasn't—" Another stab cut off her words.

"Humans cannot be trusted."

"Not all humans are the same. You told me yourself that rogue dragons probably killed our soldiers. These are rogue humans. They don't speak for the rest of us."

"Who is behind this?"

"Give me time. We'll discover the answer."

"It is because I released the Cabot boy. He raised this attack on my wing!"

"No, it wasn't Lukas. He was with me. He fought to save your yellow mother. He captured the attackers."

She felt Rory's acknowledgment and was grateful.

"It has long been known the Cabots are no friend of dragons, and if Rosa spoke truthfully, they are no friend of the humans either," Brindisi said.

"Most of the villagers don't agree with the actions of the chancellor, that's true. Many people will welcome the dragons to Olmerta. We need time to root out the offenders."

The voice, and thankfully the pain, was gone. Ashton sat up, feeling nauseous. She saw Rory watching her. "I don't know what happened," she said.

"Brindisi doesn't trust easily. She was hopeful because you are Rosa's granddaughter."

"But she can trust me!" Ashton insisted.

"For your sake, I hope so," Rory said. With that, he lifted off and was gone.

Chapter 32

Ashton saw a small dot on the horizon as she walked across the field toward Olmerta. It came on at great speed until she was able to make out the shape of Lukas on horseback.

He reined to a stop in front of her and jumped from his saddle, grabbing her in a bearhug without speaking.

She let herself relax in his arms and released the tears she'd been holding. When she finally pulled away, she saw he had been crying too.

"What are you crying about?" she asked in a teasing tone.

"You need to stop running off like that. When Sheba showed up with an arrow in her saddlebag, Galileo had a relapse."

She grabbed his forearms. "Is he okay? I need to get to him."

"He'll be fine. A little shaken, but once he sees you, all will be right again. What happened?"

Shaking her head, she relayed all that had transpired. In the end, she held up a piece of metal. "This was on one of the bodies."

Lukas took the insignia. "This is the symbol of the chancellor's personal guard."

"Imagine that," she said sarcastically.

He was stupefied.

"I guess letting the chancellor know wasn't such a great idea," she said. Seeing the look of distress on his face, she wrapped her arms around him. "You couldn't have known."

He turned abruptly, breaking free from her hold. "I have some things to discuss with the chancellor."

"Hold on now, Lukas. I don't think that's a good plan. We need to come up with another way."

He climbed into the saddle and reached down for her. "If you want a ride, let's get going."

She sighed as she settled herself into place behind him, encircling his waist with her arms.

There was no talking to him as they rode under the cloud of his brooding silence.

When they arrived in Galileo's yard, the old man rushed out to greet them. He wept tears of joy at seeing Ashton safe. His thick arms smothered her as he rocked her as he had when she was a child.

When she finally released herself from his grasp, she turned to thank Lukas, but it was too late. He and Zephyr were gone.

Her grandfather ushered her into the cottage, and Ashton filled him in on the fate of the mother and her eggs. Galileo was burning with anger. She rarely saw him this way.

"It's time," he declared.

"Time for what?"

"The people need to rise up. We need to band together against the chancellor and his cruel ways."

"What can we do? We don't have soldiers," Ashton asked.

"A blazing fire may scorch the ground, but a consistent river can move a mountain."

She tilted her head and gave him a questioning look.

"Think of something else. The villagers outnumber the soldiers," Galileo said, exasperated. "We don't have to fight the same way as the chancellor. We shouldn't! But we need to keep the dragons safe. And we need the village on our side."

"What do you need me to do?"

"Let's get to the shop. We'll gather some people along the way."

Ashton grabbed bread and cheese from the table and stuffed them in a sack. She had a feeling it would be a while before she would have a chance to eat anything.

They took a circuitous route through town, stopping along the way at cottages where Galileo spoke rapidly before hurrying on to the next. Shortly after they arrived at the shop, people began showing up. When the crowd gathered, Galileo stepped up on an old crate and raised his hands for silence.

Eventually, the chatting ceased, and they gave him their attention.

"This better not be another one of your crazy stories, Galileo," someone said from the rear.

"The dragons need us," her grandfather said.

"Oh, here we go again," another voice rang out.

"They don't want to harm us," he insisted.

"Tell that to poor Frankel," someone said.

"Frankel already knows." Frankel pushed through the crowd to join Galileo at the front. The crowd parted, whispering and pointing. "Yes, I'm alive and in one piece. It was all a misunderstanding."

"Ha! That's rich. How can a creature like that understand or misunderstand? I think the event has traumatized you."

To Ashton's eyes, Frankel looked as if he had put on weight in the short time since she had seen him last. He had shaved his beard, and his face was darker than usual. There was a sparkle in his eyes as he addressed the crowd.

"As you can see, I am no worse for the wear. I visited with the queen and her wing for a time." At this, he looked at Ashton. "We came to an agreement."

The people stirred uncomfortably.

"They have no wish to harm me or any of you. They picked me up . . . for a chat."

"How ridiculous!" someone muttered.

"If the concept of dragons is believable to you, why not communication with them?" Frankel asked.

No one answered, so he went on. "The dragons used to live in peace with the humans here in Olmerta. Something went wrong. We," he gestured to Galileo and Ashton, "want to make it right. That will only work with your help."

"Last night, some people attacked a dragon on the sands of Silent Lake. It was an unprovoked attack, and I was there to witness it," Ashton said.

"Why was there a dragon at the lake?" someone asked.

"They need to come here to lay eggs, so their young are born healthy," Ashton said. "We don't understand the science behind it, but we have seen the results."

"They've done this before?!" a tall man in the front cried in outrage. "They're multiplying!"

"And what a blessing that is." Master Gena's voice rang out across the room.

Many in the room bowed their heads automatically in the presence of the very well-respected scholar.

"These creatures have returned to us in a time of great need—ours, not theirs."

Whispers broke out. The master scholar waited for silence.

"The crops have been failing. We all know that. The taxes are going up as our production is going down. It must come to an end."

"What does that have to do with dragons?" a woman asked, bouncing a toddler on her hip.

"The dragons have something we can use to improve our yield," Gena said.

Ashton and Galileo exchanged a curious look.

Gena reached into her robe and pulled out two red, round fruits. She held them high for all to see. One was twice the size of the other. "I picked these from my garden this morning."

"But that's not possible; it isn't the season."

"And yet I hold them in my hand," she said. "And note the size. One was fertilized by something we can only get from the dragons."

"Feces?" came a voice from the back. Uneasy laughter rippled through the crowd.

"Well, I haven't tested that, but it's worth a try," Gena said with a smile. "No, I used the eggshells from ripened and hatched dragon eggs found on the shore of Silent Lake. It will take some more experimenting to get the mixture right, but I think, with the help of the dragons, we can get our crops and our prosperity back once again."

Now the throng was bubbling with excitement.

"How do we get our hands on these eggshells?" a man asked.

"That's just it. They must be given to us freely from the dragons. It isn't something we can take from them," Gena said.

"The dragons want to come to the lake," Ashton joined in. "They need to be unhindered. The attacks must be stopped."

"It doesn't take much of an imagination to guess who would want to keep us from thriving," the woman with the toddler said. "As long as we are working day and night, we can't cause trouble for the palace."

"But doesn't our prosperity mean more money for the chancellor as well?" someone asked.

"Maybe he hasn't seen that logic yet. It's up to us to guide him in that direction," Gena said.

Chapter 33

The air was only slightly fresher than the last time Gena was here with Lukas. With so little air flow this far underground, there was still a lingering odor of the cheese they had snacked on.

From her last visit, she had a pretty good idea where to look for the information she needed. She lifted the lantern high to read the titles on the tomes on the upper racks.

She tripped over something, and it skittered across the floor. Lowering her light, she saw the overturned contents of a nearby crate, now reduced to broken pottery, glass, and metal beads glittering in a potpourri of waste.

Her scholarly heart broke to see such useless disregard for these treasures. It took all her restraint to not immediately clean the mess and put things to right. She knew she had to leave it the way she found it if her visit was to go unnoticed. *But who had been down here if the vaults were supposed to be off-limits? It could only be the chancellor. Or his lap dog.*

She was fairly certain neither would understand the value of history.

She pulled down a thick record book with dates stamped on the spine. These were the latest dates in the vault. Later volumes were kept in her own library, available to all. *Why the change?*

A puzzle for another time. For now, she wanted to check the ledger to confirm a theory. No one would miss this book taken from a library long abandoned.

Bayard slipped in quietly through the door behind the throne.

"They're in the dungeon being guarded by soldiers," he informed Nikolai.

"Have they spoken?" the chancellor asked.

"Not a word."

"Kill them."

"The soldiers as well?" Bayard asked.

"Unless you can think of another way to get to them."

Bayard stood silently until Nikolai turned on him. "What?"

"We have the master scholar. She was found snooping around outside the vaults again."

The chancellor's eyes burned through Bayard. "Did she get in?"

"No, the guards stopped her and brought her to me."

Letting out a deep breath, he said, "Bring her in."

Master Gena walked with her head held high, guards flanking her. When she reached the dais, she bowed her head quickly, with no reverence.

"I hear you've been looking for a way into the vault. Maybe you didn't get the message the first time, Gena."

She stared him down.

"Master Gena," he said, dripping with sarcasm.

"My duty to Olmerta includes research and education. It hasn't been that long since you were learning in my care, but it seems you have forgotten some of your manners."

"I don't need lectures from dried-up old teachers. Explain why you were trying to get in the vaults."

She stood tall with her hands clasped comfortably in front of her robes. "I'm trying to discover why the dragons have returned to the city and how we can use it to our advantage."

That got his attention. "And what have you found?"

"Nothing concrete yet. I do believe there is a connection between crop yield and the dragons' eggs. I need to do more study."

"And what does that entail?"

"I would like to see if there is mention of when the dragons were last seen in Olmerta and the records of crop production to see if there is a correlation. For that, I need access to the vault."

"Is that all?"

"I need the dragons to lay eggs on the sands of Silent Lake," she said without emotion.

Nikolai's eyes danced. "And you need soldiers to capture the eggs for you?"

She shook her head as if disappointed in her pupil. "No. The eggs need to hatch healthy. I need the shells."

"So the shells have some value?" He shifted in his seat.

"That is yet to be seen. That is why I need to study them."

"When will there be another hatching?"

"That is for the dragons to know, not us."

"I shall post guards to ensure no ruffians disturb your study—at the beach and your cottage."

She nodded her head in acknowledgment. "Once I have something to study." *Thankfully I have the most important records from my last trip.*

"A guard will escort you to the vault. You may search the tomes only. Leave everything else undisturbed. You will show me all your notes, so write in a real language, not that drivel you usually use."

She turned to leave, muttering, "Seems like this dried-up old teacher still has some usefulness."

Chapter 34

Ashton turned the sign in the shop window to read closed for any passersby. The streetlamps were glowing, but their light didn't quite reach into the corners and alleyways.

She took her seat in the room next to Lukas as Master Gena paced in front of the small group. Galileo sat on Ashton's other side.

"I'm nearby," she heard Rory speak to her. "If you share with me, I can hear their words."

"Rory's listening," Ashton said. "I think we're all ready." She invited Master Gena to begin.

"I made another trip to the vault."

"How did you—"

Gena cut Lukas off. "A story for another time. Let's just say, I predicted we might need an extra key, so I made an impression before the guards took it away." She continued addressing the group. "The record vault was sealed soon after the Cabots came to power. They didn't want anyone to learn of their betrayal."

"What do you mean, came to power? What betrayal?" Lukas asked.

She looked directly at him. "We were right. Olmerta was once ruled by a queen. I'm sorry, Lukas, but the Cabots overthrew the monarchy."

He shook his head. "Why? What reason would they have?"

"The Cabots took over for the power and the money. From what I could gather, they used the villagers' displeasure over the non-yielding crops and the dragons to seize power from the queen's rule."

"What crop?" Galileo asked.

Master Gena opened the book to a page with a drawing of a feathery, red plant.

"I saw those growing inside the mountain," Ashton said. "It's what we mixed with lake water to make the paste."

"At one time, it grew wild in this area, but it's useless to humans, so they dug it up and planted other crops. When the dragons started to get sick, one of our earliest queens realized the plant was something the dragons needed in their diet. She directed all farmers to use a percentage of their land to grow more." Gena was warming to her subject as if by saying it out loud, all the pieces were falling into place.

"They figured out the properties from the eggshells by chance when someone moved them from the lakeshore to decorate their home garden. It turned into a symbiotic relationship. Healthy dragons meant more hatchings."

Ashton finished the thought. "Which meant more eggshells that increased the production yield."

Gena nodded. "As generations passed, the farmers grew greedy. They wanted to decrease the farming of what they considered to be a useless crop. Queen Ashlea noted in a journal that Sir Richard

Cabot approached her with the idea of culling the dragon's numbers. She forbade any harm to them."

Gena referred to her documents. "After that, many villagers approached the throne, demanding the same idea that Cabot had brought forth. They were convinced if there weren't so many dragons, they could grow cash crops in those fields instead.

"When the queen still refused, the Cabots instigated an uprising against the royal family. A loyal historian detailed the events using an old language lost to most but the scholars. I found it on my second trip to the archives when I knew where to look."

Gena sunk into a chair, resting her hands on her lap. "Once the queen and many of her family members were killed, there was no one to stop the hunting of dragons."

Ashton put her hand on Lukas's clenched fists. Gena went on, oblivious to his discomfort.

"Oh, some families tried, but they couldn't get the masses to listen to them. When Queen Ashlea was killed, the connection to the dragon community was severed."

"Brindisi spoke of how painful the loss was when my grandmother died. It left her despondent and empty, like some part of her was missing. Maybe the same thing happened with the queens," Ashton said.

"That special bond was not only between the queens," Gena said. "Other members of the royal family had made connections. If they all suffered the same fate, can you imagine what kind of state the dragons would be in?"

The group was quiet as the thought sunk in.

The master scholar cleared her throat and went on. "Weapons were designed and forged specifically for hunting the dragons, and the villagers made a sport of it. The Cabot family made money selling these weapons to neighboring villages, claiming the weapons were for their safety."

Galileo spoke quietly. "After suffering many casualties, I suppose the dragons decided to leave Olmerta, not wanting anything to do with the humans."

"Agreed," Gena said. "And without the eggshells from the dragon hatchings, the crops began to suffer. Slowly at first, so the cause wasn't immediately connected, but if you look over history, the production yield has become less than half of what it had been. And the size of the fruits is reportedly much smaller than what the records show from the time of the dragons."

"Some humans came to the mountain with us," Rory said. Ashton jumped, having forgotten he was listening. "A few could still speak with us. They planted what we needed within our mountain."

Ashton relayed what Rory was saying to the others.

He went on. "They were free to come and go, but they were sworn to tell no one where we were. Some of the young ones stayed until adulthood, but then they left to find mates. Eventually, the last of that group succumbed to old age. It was many, many years before Rosa came to the mountain."

She finished vocalizing for him, then asked, "Has Brindisi been alive that whole time?"

"Healthy dragons live much longer than a human can imagine, but no, this Brindisi is daughter to the queen of your discussion."

"She was named after her mother?" she asked.

Ashton felt the chuckle. "Brindisi is a title, like your queen. She leads us all."

"And the dragons have been living in the mountain ever since," Lukas said in wonder.

"Why did they come back now?" Ashton chimed in.

"I believe your grandmother Rosa had a suspicion where they went. She went to check a theory," Gena said.

"But why didn't she come home once she found them?" Ashton said.

"Rosa came home once," Galileo said. "She was excited but very cryptic about where she had been or what she had found. She said she needed to leave again for a short time but would return and tell me everything. She only needed more supplies. Your grandmother was a capable woman and headstrong. I knew she would share her discoveries with me when she could."

He took Ashton's hand in his. "When months had gone by and she didn't return, your parents went looking for her." A tear slid down his face. "Their bodies were found near the foothills."

"It was probably the guards my uncle had stationed there to keep people from reconnecting with the dragons," Lukas growled.

"But how did the chancellor know about the dragons?" Ashton asked.

"I don't think he did," Gena said. "He was probably following the same protocols as his ancestors. He was taught the foothills must remain impassable, so that's what he did. Not a lot of original ideas from the Cabots."

Lukas's face turned red, and anger flashed in his eyes. Gena was oblivious still.

Galileo kept speaking to Ashton. "When your parents died, I stopped looking for Rosa. I had more pressing things to attend to." He squeezed her hand.

A tear slid down Ashton's cheek. Lukas shifted to put his arms around her and let her rest on his shoulder.

"Tell us the rest," Galileo prompted Gena.

"After the Cabots took control and created the chancellor position—"

"—But treated it like royalty, passed from generation to generation within their family line," Lukas cut in.

Gena nodded. "The crops continued to decline, but the people made money from the sales of weapons. Before long, there were other things to concern them, and the memory of the dragons passed away."

"Now what do we do?" Lukas asked.

Ashton sat up. "We help the dragons. That's what Grandma Rosa wanted. Everything else is in the past. Let's leave it there."

"That means getting them access to the lake without being harassed," Galileo said.

Lukas shook his head. "I spoke to Nikolai. He denies everything. Even when I showed him the insignia, he said ruffians must have stolen the gear and been hiding out in the foothills, knowing people wouldn't look for them there. He claims he'll investigate it."

"What about the attack at the lake?" Ashton asked.

"He says he knew nothing about it and wants the offenders punished immediately."

"Of course he does," Ashton muttered under her breath.

"The people support us," Galileo said.

"So we start another uprising? Is that really what we need right now?" Ashton said. "Besides, we have no proof Nikolai was behind this."

"We need to bring the dragons here again," Galileo said.

"Why would the dragons trust us at this point?" She focused her question at Rory but spoke it aloud.

"They are weary. Brindisi is angry," she heard him reply. "We must tread carefully from here."

"Why don't we start by planting what they need?" Galileo said.

"We need to get the farmers onboard. They'd have to give up some land again," Ashton said.

"What's Nikolai going to say when he hears they are planting a non-profit crop?" Lukas said.

"Leave the farmers to me," Galileo said. "But I think it would go a long way if they could meet the dragons themselves. Can you ask your friend if that's possible?"

"They cannot come to the mountain," Rory said. "We'll have to find another way."

Chapter 35

Ashton sat atop Sheba on the outskirts of town, ready to lead the select group of twenty villagers to meet with the dragons. Excitement was in the air, mixed with a touch of nervousness. She understood completely. She felt the same way the first time she traveled through the foothills of the Silent Mountain.

She raised her voice to speak to the gathering. "Remember, not all dragons can communicate with humans and not all humans can hear the dragons. Be patient and don't be afraid."

They set off with their horses at a quick walk, people chatting and visiting between groups. Ashton listened to them speculating what the creatures would be like, all hoping they'd be one of the lucky able to communicate with them.

Lukas rode up to her. "We're in place. My soldiers scouted the woods, and I didn't see any signs of Nikolai's guards. He may have pulled them after the failed attack on you."

"Good. We're setting a good pace and can make it to the bridge before the second sun sets," she said.

"Have you heard from Rory?"

"Not yet. I don't think we're close enough. He knows we're coming. I hope he was able to convince some of the others to join him."

"What if Brindisi doesn't let them?"

She shrugged. "She wants what's best for her wing. I don't know what other choice she has."

They continued in silence until they neared the forest at the foothills. Rory interrupted her thoughts. "We'll be ready."

Ashton sighed with relief and smiled at Lukas. "Rory came through."

As they came to the spot where the mother dragon had lost her eggs, sadness overtook Ashton. She saw the burnt grass but nothing else remained. A little farther away, scorched bits of metal were the only thing left of Nikolai's personal guard who once terrorized the foothills to keep people from reconnecting with the dragons.

Now they needed people with the ability to communicate with the wing. Master Gena couldn't find any concrete studies as to why some people could hear them while others couldn't, so they were conducting their own. They had rounded up farmers throughout Olmerta who were willing to meet with the dragons. After Gena's persuasive speech at Galileo's shop, more than enough stepped forward. They had to draw lots to see who got to make the first trip.

The path through the woods was narrow, and the gaggle had to ride single file most of the way. They made enough noise to keep the wild animals at bay, and Ashton didn't have the feeling of being watched this time. Having traveled this path before, she was much more relaxed and looked forward to what awaited them in the clearing.

As they rode, Ashton watched Lukas's back. When had it become so broad? He constantly moved his head, scanning the path and woods ahead. She noted his hair was getting rather long and would need trimming soon.

She shook her head, laughing out loud. Lukas turned in the saddle to face her. "What's so funny?"

"I'm laughing at myself. When did we grow up?"

He gave her a quizzical look. "I think it's been happening over time."

"Did you ever imagine when Galileo told us his stories that we'd be in one?"

He turned and faced front again. "As long as it has a good ending."

They had made good time, and the first sun was only now lowering over the mountain. Following Lukas into the clearing, she saw Rory perched near the canyon as if he were royalty himself.

She looked around but didn't see any others from the wing.

"This needs to be a gradual process," Rory told her, and she saw the sense in it.

As the riders emerged, they fanned out to the left and right of her and Lukas. They were stunned into silence at the sight of Rory in his splendid beauty of shimmering steely-blue.

Playing his part well, Rory bowed his head by way of greeting. Then he looked down the row of humans, one by one. Ashton could tell by their reactions when he came across one who could hear him. And by the disappointment on their faces when Rory's gaze passed by those without any connection.

In the end, only three out of the twenty riders made a connection with Rory, but Ashton counted it as a victory that all could see him.

"More come," Rory told her.

She spoke to the crowd. "More dragons are arriving. Prepare your horses so they don't spook."

Some riders got out of their saddles and took the reins in front, stroking their horse's nose with calming words.

A warm wind buffeted the group, announcing the arrival of three more dragons of various shades. Ashton recognized at least one of them from a discolored scale on its chest. She had seen him in the cave. Upon closer inspection, she spotted other nuances about each dragon that made it unique from the others. As Rory gave their names, Ashton committed them to memory as she studied them physically and felt their minds.

This time when the dragons spoke, two more joined those who could hear them. Ashton laughed as they spoke out loud, then stopped midsentence as the dragon explained *sentsentia* to them.

While the other humans were disappointed, they were excited for the chance to see these beautiful creatures and learn more about them.

Before the second sun was gone completely, Lukas called for everyone to set up camp for the night. The villagers quickly complied, anxious to get through this task and back to the dragons. Ashton watched as they worked together setting up camp, but also as those who could communicate with the dragons asked questions on behalf of those who could not.

"It's going well, don't you think?" Lukas asked, startling her.

She smiled. "Better than I could have hoped for."

He put a hand on her shoulder. "You pulled it off."

"We did. I wish Galileo could have been here to see it."

"He isn't in any shape to travel," he said. "He's getting on in years and has had a few too many shocks lately."

"I know. It's hard for me to remember he's growing up too."

When the dragons left for the night, the villagers gathered around a fire. There were so many conversations going on at once, Ashton couldn't concentrate. She heard several discussing plans to rotate the crops so they could make room for the dragon fire, which is what the villagers had begun calling the red plant their new friends needed.

Eventually, Lukas shooed everyone off to their bedrolls. They needed to get to Olmerta tomorrow, which meant getting a decent start in the morning. He stretched out on his bedroll with his head next to Ashton's.

"Everything's going to change," she whispered.

Chapter 36

The villagers immediately spread the word about their visit with the dragons. Their excitement caught on, and soon others were seeking out Ashton and Lukas to see when they could take their turn.

The Silent Mountain Shop was busier than ever. Galileo hardly had time to work on new creations and had orders that would take him months to fill.

Lukas was training new recruits and reevaluating everyone under his charge. Having one turncoat in their midst sprinkled seeds of doubt over everyone else.

Farmers immediately set to work planting the dragon fire Ashton and Lukas had retrieved from the mountain. It would take a season for the plant to take solid root, but they were on their way toward making the dragon wing feel more welcome.

There were still holdouts who harassed Galileo at the marketplace and complained about planting for the dragons when there was a lack of food for humans. Even Master Gena gave up trying to explain the tradeoff with them.

The bells above the door jingled. Ashton looked up to see Lukas's grinning face.

"What has put you in such a good mood?" she asked.

"You'll never believe it. Uncle Nikolai wants to encourage the return of the dragons."

"What? You're right. I don't believe it. What changed his mind?"

"Maybe he's finally listening to me. I've been talking to him about what we've learned—"

"You didn't tell him about the mountain, did you?"

Lukas's face fell. "Do you find me that simple?"

She placed a hand on his arm. "No. I'm sorry. You told him what we learned about what?"

Too excited to stand still, he paced the room, talking with his hands.

"I told him how much good the eggshells could do for Olmerta. Think of the increase in revenue from the surge in plant production! Master Gena agreed with me, although she wasn't very happy that I had gone to him before warning her. She had already told him her theory, so I'm not sure what she was upset about."

Ashton gave him a sideways look.

"What did I do?" Lukas asked.

Picking up a rag, Ashton proceeded to wipe the shelves as she spoke. "Remember Master Gena mentioning that the Cabots took over because of the money and power?"

"Well, sure, but that was ages ago . . ." he trailed off.

"If all you and your uncle are concerned about is making more money from the dragons, maybe we are creating another problem."

Lukas shook his head. Frustrated, he couldn't find the words to explain what he was trying to do.

"We need Uncle Nikolai on our side. At least not against us. I'm trying to help."

She stopped polishing long enough to look at him. "You are helping. None of this would work without you. We need to be careful, that's all. We're still trying to get Brindisi to trust us again."

"And you don't think having Uncle Nikolai aiding us will help that?"

"I'm not sure what I believe right now. There are too many unanswered questions."

"Thanks for ruining my good mood." Lukas left the shop without another word, even when Ashton called after him.

They waited on the beach, not sure if a dragon would arrive. The pit was dug, and soldiers stood guard, their backs to the water as they faced any possible danger from the trees.

Finally Ashton felt the warm breeze when Rory landed. His large head swiveled as he took in the soldiers. "Do you think this is wise?"

"They're Lukas's men and women. Your dragon is safe. Who's coming?"

"Midas comes. I wanted to verify the conditions for myself first."

Within moments, a dragon heavy with eggs came to rest near the prepared pit. "Thank you," Ashton heard within her mind. She also felt the nervousness and wariness.

"This is his fourth hatching," Rory offered. "None have lived long."

The idea of so much loss hurt Ashton. She glanced at the soldiers and hoped Lukas was right about his choices. Then she chastised herself for doubting him.

"You are welcome, Midas. Let us pray for health and long life for your dragonettes."

Midas approached the pit. He froze when a wracking pain hit him. When he could move again, he positioned himself to lay the eggs in the prepared sand.

Ashton stepped away to talk to Master Gena and Lukas.

"Who is this?" Gena asked, her parchment and pen at the ready.

"Midas. This is his fourth hatching. No luck with the others."

Gena scribbled down the information. "For all our sakes, let's hope things go better for him this time."

Lukas didn't so much as smile when Ashton approached. "How are things going with training?" Ashton asked.

"We have fine soldiers. More being groomed all the time."

Master Gena cleared her throat. "I'm going to make sure the carts are ready."

"They're in position. My team put them where you asked," Lukas said.

"Yes," she glanced at Ashton, then at Lukas. "I appreciate it, but I should see for myself."

"Are you still mad at me?" Ashton asked when they were alone.

"Mad? Why would I be?" He still didn't look at her, his eyes constantly scanning the forest.

"This is ridiculous." She grabbed his arm, forcing him to face her. "How can you be angry because I expressed doubts?"

"You don't believe I'm capable of doing my job, something I've been trained to do my whole life. Why would that possibly bother me?"

She broke eye contact first.

When she heard shuffling on the beach, she returned to the pit. Rory and Midas were using their hind legs to kick sand over the eggs. She watched them finish, then went to retrieve the unused shovel. "Guess we won't be needing these anymore."

Rory nodded. "There was a time before humans when dragons managed on their own."

"I know. It's good to be needed though. Do you want us to keep dragon fire nearby for the pit?"

"We have ensured the wing members closest to clutching feed heartily from the plant. We believe that is the best way to supply the nutrients to the eggs," he said.

He spread his wings. "Keep the eggs safe until hatching."

"We will. We'll have someone on guard around the clock."

"As will I," Midas said. "I am not leaving."

Ashton placed a hand on Midas's front talon. "Rest now."

He laid his huge head between his front feet, his snout on top of the sand covering his eggs.

Ashton walked to where she had left Lukas, but he had moved on.

Chapter 37

Gena knew the hatching would be any day now. Her young students were working quietly on their letters at the table in her front room. She took the opportunity to create new charts for the distribution of the eggshells.

Because she couldn't predict the number of eggs or even the number of dragons who would lay a clutch, she couldn't guarantee a share to anyone. The best she could do was design a priority list. She started with the farmers who had already planted dragon fire. Next, she included the ones who had plans to add the red plant to the fields after their harvest.

She hesitated over the next set of names. What about those who refused to support the dragons? Should they also be considered? They were part of Olmerta, but if they weren't willing to sacrifice for the good of the dragons, why should they profit?

Laying her pen aside, she decided she needed time to ponder this situation more carefully. She walked through the pupils, pointing out corrections here and there, sometimes answering questions.

The door flew open. An excited soldier stood before the class. "Master Gena, your presence is requested. It's time."

The children started talking all at once, excited themselves at the big news. Everyone in town knew a hatching was taking place on the beach.

"Settle down now," Gena said. "Pack up your things. Leave your areas neat. That's right." Although eager to leave herself, her first responsibility was to her young charges. When at last they finished, she ushered them out of the cottage and toward their homes.

Gena gave a sign for the impatient soldier to follow, and she rushed toward the lake.

The sight was not what she expected. The soldiers were busy but not in defending the dragon's clutch. They held a strict cordon to keep onlookers away from the hatching ground as more and more poured from the village.

Her escort pushed through the crowd, making a path for the master scholar. When the people became aware of her presence, they bowed their heads in respect and went silent, at least until she passed. Then the chatter started up again.

Rory had returned and stood watching the humans as Midas dug sand carefully from the pit. Gena appreciated his wariness. She was a little uncomfortable herself, especially after last time. The good news was that this crowd seemed joyous, not hostile.

Gena approached Ashton and Galileo inside the circle. Ashton bounced on her toes as if she couldn't stand still. Galileo was all smiles, not able to tear his eyes away from the pit.

Pulling out her parchment, Gena began to draw the placement of the eggs and noted the color. This seemed to be a small clutch, with only three eggs. The first crack appeared in the yellow oval. It rocked to and fro, becoming more frantic with each pivot. Finally, a burst of gooey wings and beak broke free.

Midas immediately reached in and scooped the dragonette out of the hole. The baby stretched its wings, the slimy substance dripping away as the dragon shook and stumbled toward the water.

Gena was so enamored by the sight, she was surprised she had missed the second hatching. A blue dragonette was now struggling to free itself from the muck covering its scales. Midas gave it a gentle nudge, causing it to topple over. In its efforts to right itself, much of the substance was brushed away by the sand.

Very ingenious. Gena scribbled furiously.

When she looked into the pit, the third egg was barely moving. Hairline fractures covered the top of the egg, but no holes had broken through. Her heart ached.

Midas's attention was split between watching his two dragonettes waddle toward the water and glancing into the pit. His giant head swung toward Rory, then as if in agreement, Rory followed the young ones to the water while Midas concentrated on the last egg. He nuzzled it with his large snout, breathing warm air over the surface.

Midas used his front talon to gently tap the shell. Gena was surprised at the gentleness of such a large creature. A tiny hole appeared. Then the egg began to rock violently. In no time, the egg burst open and a tiny gold dragonette popped out.

Ashton and Galileo released a sigh of relief. It wasn't until then that Gena realized she had also been holding her breath.

The gold dragon waddled to join the others, with Midas close behind. The dragonettes were already diving under the water and coming up with tasty treats. When the family was together, Rory returned to the sand.

"Rory says Midas is beside himself with joy. His hatchings have never gone this well," Ashton relayed.

As Gena inventoried the eggshells, a hush fell over the crowd. She looked up to see what could have silenced the throng. Many were dispersing in haste when the chancellor was let through the cordon. Lukas jogged over from his station to address his uncle.

He bowed from the waist with a salute. "You missed the joyous hatching, sir. But as you can see, the dragonettes are well."

"How many shells are there?" Nikolai asked without even regarding the water where the babies fished and played.

"Three eggs, Chancellor," Gena said.

"And how many fields do you think they can supplement?"

"I'm still working the calculations, but probably three plots once they are properly ground and proportioned."

"How much will that increase the yield?"

"It's too early to tell. I still have to do a lot more experimenting."

He beckoned to his personal guards. "Collect the shells." To Gena, he said, "I expect a recommendation on the sale price by the end of the day."

"Chancellor Nikolai, the eggshells have been promised to farmers who are planting the dragon fire," Gena said.

"You shouldn't make promises you have no authority to affect." Nikolai yanked the reins to turn his horse away from the pit.

"Uncle, Master Gena is working on a system to ensure fair and equitable disposition of the shells," Lukas said.

"The disposition will be determined by the coins in their purse." Nikolai rode off without another glance.

Chapter 38

"Are you kidding me?" Ashton cried out. "Leave it to the Cabots to swoop in and take something that doesn't belong to them to line their pockets."

Lukas spun to face her. "The chancellor is only one of the Cabots."

"This is your fault," she spat. "If you hadn't suggested the value of the eggshells, Nikolai wouldn't have given us a second thought."

"If I hadn't convinced him of the worth of the dragons, he would have mustered his soldiers to kill them!"

"Have *you* kill them, you mean! And you would have followed orders, like the good little soldier you are."

Galileo stepped between the two, placing a hand on their shoulders. "Take a breath. This is a bump in the road; it isn't the end."

Lukas roughly shook off Galileo's touch. "I have *orders* to follow." He stomped toward the village.

Ashton was still steaming. Arms across her chest, she couldn't seem to compose herself. She felt Rory's nudge inside her head, but she pushed him away.

"How did you do that?" Galileo asked.

"Do what?" she said.

"Rory said you blocked him out."

Ashton blinked and refocused her energy. "I don't know. I didn't do it intentionally."

This time, she opened her mind. "Sorry, Rory. I was angry, but not at you."

"What caused your anger? You turned red hot. Brindisi gets that way at times."

"The chancellor has confiscated the eggshells."

She felt the confusion from Rory.

"We wanted to use the shells to help the farmers who are helping the dragons. Nikolai wants to sell the shells to make a profit. He doesn't care about the dragon fire."

"Brindisi warned you about the Cabots. Nothing good comes from them."

Galileo broke into their conversation. "Ashton, you were too harsh on Lukas. He's doing his best to help, like we all are."

She shrugged.

"The first milestone was reached. There was a successful hatching without an attack. Let's celebrate this birth and then turn our attention toward the next problem."

"Your grandfather is right," Master Gena said from behind Ashton. "Perhaps I can convince the chancellor that it's too soon to charge for a product when we aren't assured of its value. That way I can continue my studies."

A shower of water droplets hit them as the dragon family flew over them, lake water dripping from their wings.

"I will escort Midas and his young ones to the mountain. Brindisi will be anxious to hear about the hatching," Rory said.

Galileo put his arm on Ashton's shoulders. "Why don't we fill in the pit? Master Gena has work to do, I'm certain. Then we'll round up something to eat."

She let him guide her to the shovels. The simple exertion cleared her head, and she began to feel guilty about what she had said to Lukas. She knew he wasn't like his uncle, but she couldn't seem to let the facts tame her emotions.

"Why is the chancellor all about money?" She stabbed the spade into the sand, adding another scoop to the pit.

"It's not possible to trace his motives. At one time, I may have been able to talk to him, but now he's a stranger."

She stopped and stared at her grandfather. "Wait a minute. Are you saying you were once friends?"

"That was another age, long forgotten." He tossed a final load to finish covering the hole.

"You can't leave it like that," Ashton said. "What happened?"

Galileo stuck the shovel into the sand and leaned on the handle. "Nikolai fancied your grandmother a while."

"He what?!"

Galileo chuckled. "That's right. He followed Rosa around when he was under Master Gena's training and Rosa was assisting her. Lucky for me, Rosa liked more mature men."

Ashton plopped down in the sand, unable to believe her ears. "Why have you never told me this story?"

"It isn't much of a story to tell. Nikolai was quite taken with Rosa. She was bright, funny, and beautiful. Every man had an eye on her."

He took a handkerchief from his pocket and mopped his brow. "Much like now, Nikolai felt he

221

deserved things, rather than having to earn them. When she didn't return his affections—which would have been ridiculous with their age difference—he was furious."

"Did he come after you?"

He waved his hand. "He was never so direct. Besides, I was much older and bigger than he was. It wouldn't have been much of a fight without his guards on his side."

Ashton shook her head. This was a whole new side of her grandparents she had never explored. She smiled to think of Galileo as a young man trying to impress Rosa.

"Enough of this," he said. "I'm famished. Let's have dinner at the inn. I need to stop at the shop so I can pick up the work I was doing before the hatching interrupted me." He held out a hand and hauled Ashton to her feet.

By the time they had reached town, an angry mob had gathered outside the Silent Mountain Shop. They began shouting as soon as they saw Ashton and Galileo approach.

"Those eggshells were supposed to be ours!" someone yelled.

"Why should we plant dragon fire if we aren't getting anything in return?" another cried.

"Calm down, calm down." Galileo pushed his way through to open the door. "We'll figure this out."

"Perhaps we should take the shells ourselves!"

"No!" Ashton said. "We cannot let this turn into a physical altercation. The chancellor's personal guards are armed. We must find another way to settle this."

"We have the soldiers, do we not?" a man said.

"Forget the soldiers; we have dragons!"

A cheer went up in the crowd.

Ashton cringed. She wasn't sure where the soldiers stood on this matter. They still took their directions from the chancellor, as well as their pay. Even though many supported the return of the dragons and had family members who still farmed the land, it was hard to gauge where their loyalties would fall.

She was even less sure of the dragons' willingness to help humans.

"We don't want a war in Olmerta," Ashton said.

The crowd funneled into the shop and filled the space. They quieted, waiting for Galileo to give them reassurances.

"The chancellor is the ruler of Olmerta," he couched.

"More like the dictator!" came the response.

Galileo raised his hands to calm the people before they got riled up again. "Either way, he's in charge. We have to be wise. No one do anything rash. We'll figure this out together."

"Have the dragons pay him a visit!" This was followed by cheers and clapping.

Ashton spoke up. "I will go to the dragons and tell them our situation. I'm not guaranteeing they will help."

"Remind them we have the dragon fire," someone suggested. "We can as easily burn it as plant it."

Ashton didn't like this change in attitude. It was as if the villagers had forgotten what got them to this point to begin with. She wanted to mend the breach, not make threats. One thing she was sure of: Brindisi would not be motivated through coercion.

Chapter 39

"But this does affect you," Ashton argued. She once again stood on the ledge inside the crystal cavern, putting her more at eye level with Brindisi.

"Humans will always squabble over what they have or have not. It is their nature," Brindisi said.

"I thought you would be more concerned. This jeopardizes the hatchings."

"I do not see it that way. Now that we know the answer to our problem with the eggs, our numbers will continue to grow."

"What if the soldiers attack?"

"Then we will defend ourselves."

"It didn't work last time."

"We restrained ourselves during our last encounter with the humans. We were weak for the sake of a few friendly villagers. We won't make the same mistake again."

Ashton tried to frame a logical argument without anger. She counted to ten, then spoke calmly through *sensentia*. "Wouldn't it be better and safer if we worked together?"

Brindisi dipped her head once. "I am not seeking conflict."

"What are you looking for?"

"For my dragons to grow stronger and healthy. To rebuild my wing for the next Brindisi."

"And we've taken that first step. Midas has three new dragonettes."

A warmth seeped into Ashton's brain. "And for that, I am grateful. Midas has had such pain."

"If you want continued success, we need to quell the uprising."

"And what would you have us do?"

Ashton placed her hands on her hips and blew out a long breath. "I don't know. I was hoping you could help me figure it out."

Brindisi repositioned herself. "Humans need to deal with their own situations."

"But it affects you!"

"Dragons can take the beach," Brindisi stated.

"That doesn't solve the problem of dragon fire."

"It will return to the land."

"But how long will that take? It would be quicker if it was planted, but the farmers can only afford to give up a field for dragon fire if their other fields grow more. They need the dragon eggshells."

"They may have them."

"But the chancellor is going to take them."

"That is a problem amongst the humans. We are doing what was asked of us. Humans must solve their own disagreements."

Ashton was tired of this circular discussion. She was getting nowhere. As she turned to leave, Brindisi spoke again. "Rory will notify you for the next hatching."

You don't need me, Ashton thought, but held it from the temperamental queen.

When Ashton emerged from the mountain, the smell of burnt flesh and acrid smoke assaulted her. Covering her nose with the sleeve of her tunic, she approached the scorched mark in the grass warily. There was nothing left to identify what had been burned.

At the scraping sound behind her, she whirled around to find Rory sitting on the ledge above the opening to the cave entrance.

"What was that?" she asked.

"Intruders."

"You killed humans?"

"They were not your friends." Rory's calm demeanor was infuriating to Ashton. "But out of respect for you, we did not eat them."

She turned to the black marking in the grass. "How do you know they weren't friends? Could you hear them?"

"No, but friends would not have tracked you through the woods hiding their presence from you."

Ashton's shaking legs gave out, and she fell into the soft grass, still staring at the ashes.

"How many?"

"Three."

"Did they wear uniforms like the soldiers?"

"No. They dressed as you dress. And they spoke quietly to each other so as not to be overheard."

Ashton warred with herself, contemplating one argument, then another. Finally, she jumped to her feet and stormed to where she had left Sheba. Ripping the reins from the branches where she had tied them, she flung herself onto the horse's back. She felt Rory reach to her, but she blocked him out.

She took the path through the forest faster than usual, kicking at Sheba's sides when she slowed down. Upon reaching the meadow, Ashton urged the horse on at an unforgiving pace.

It was deep in the night before Ashton reached her grandfather's cottage and dismounted. She removed the saddle and filled the water bucket for Sheba, then brushed her in the moonlight.

The cottage door creaked open. Galileo was illuminated by the single candle he held in front of him. "I didn't expect you until tomorrow."

She paused but didn't turn. "I didn't mean to wake you."

"What happened?"

Ashton continued her brushstrokes a little more forcefully. "The queen has no intention of getting involved. She's okay with us helping her and her wing but wants the *humans* to work out their own problems."

"Is that such a bad thing?" Galileo asked.

"But how can we stand against Chancellor Nikolai? He's unreasonable and arrogant. He doesn't even take advice from his own family."

Galileo took the brush from her hand and gently stroked Sheba. "Is it a matter of standing *against* Nikolai or standing *with* each other?"

"What does that mean?"

"All your focus is on the chancellor. If you don't like what you see, change your view."

Chapter 40

Gena schooled her face when she entered the throne room and spied Lukas in full uniform standing at Nikolai's right hand.

"Ah, Master Scholar, how kind of you to join us," Nikolai said.

She nodded her head briefly in acknowledgment without rising to the bait of his sarcasm.

"My nephew tells me you have made great strides in research about the dragons."

This time, she couldn't help but cut a look at Lukas, who remained impassive.

"I don't know what you consider great strides, Chancellor, but I am making steady progress. Mostly verifying what we already suspected about the special properties of the eggshells."

"Such as," he prompted.

"We have confirmed that something in the sand of Silent Lake helps the protective covering harden properly, enabling the dragonettes to come to term."

"And that those shells increase crop production. *That's* what I want to hear about. How many shells does it take? How often? How long do the effects last?"

"It's too early to answer those questions. We need to go through a number of harvests to collect proper data."

She took the opportunity to plant a seed of her own. "I suspect if the dragon's diet included the red, feathery plant dragon fire, they would be able to produce more eggs. That would mean more eggshells."

She let him finish the next line of reasoning—meaning more money in his coffers.

Nikolai stroked his chin. "How much of this plant is needed?"

Gena shook her head. "Another question we do not know the answer to. More studies need to be done."

"Lukas, you're Master of the Dragons. Ensure the plant is included on each farm. If they claim no space, have them overturn those nasty beets. I never liked them anyway."

Saluting, Lukas said, "Yes, sir. It will be done."

Nikolai waved a hand, dismissing both Gena and Lukas. They walked together out the door of the palace.

"Master of the Dragons? That is wonderful. It puts you in a perfect position to help us," Gena said when they were clear.

"There is no 'us.' I serve the chancellor. If you have any doubts, speak with Ashton." With that, Lukas turned toward the barracks, leaving Gena in stunned silence.

"He said what?" Ashton's voice echoed off the near-empty shop.

"I don't know what's going on between you two, but you need to fix it. You have been friends since you learned side-by-side in my classroom. Now is not the time to be breaking contact with the ruling family," Gena said.

Ashton huffed, crossing her arms. "I haven't done anything wrong. I'm not going to grovel to him because of his family. I never did it before, and I refuse to start now."

Gena gave her a disapproving look. "You are no longer a child. You must reach beyond your petty feelings."

Galileo placed his wrinkled hand on Ashton's arm, shaking it gently to make her drop her hands to her side. "You are your mother's daughter. I saw that same look in her eyes many times. Master Gena is right. We need to know what's going on inside the palace. Lukas is in the perfect spot."

"So we should use him for his position? Even if he wants nothing to do with me?"

"This is naught but a spat between you. It will pass, but we don't have time for it to play out. The good news is the farmers will be planting dragon fire. That solves one of our problems."

He turned to Gena. "Do you have any idea how fast it grows or how much we need?"

"I don't know yet. If I could see where it currently grows, that would help me determine the right soil. Since it grows inside the mountain, it must not need much sun. A trip is called for."

"No." Ashton's sharp reply brought Gena up short.

"But surely you can ask Rory, and he could ensure safe passage," Gena said.

"The dragons have made it clear. They have no desire to help us. Why should we assist them?"

"It's still in our best interests to have dragons on our shore again," Gena said.

"Think of the farmers you would be supporting," Galileo said.

"It doesn't benefit the farmers. It makes the Cabots grow richer. With riches, comes power. Power that goes to their heads."

Ashton stormed out of the shop, the jingling bell incongruous with the negative energy left behind.

Gena turned to Galileo. "What do you suggest?"

"You can't go to the mountain without a dragon talker. I don't know who followed Ashton on her last trip, but the dragons made it clear they won't tolerate intruders."

"Maybe some of the people from the first group Ashton introduced to them. Connections were established then."

"Remember, only some people talk to some dragons. It isn't an all or nothing."

"We need Rory, and someone he will listen to," she said.

"He'll reappear with the next hatching, I'm sure."

"In the meantime, can you talk to Lukas?" Gena asked. "They need to patch up this misunderstanding."

"Lukas is almost as hard-headed as Ashton. He's been keeping his distance from me as well."

"It makes me long for the time when I could make them sit at the peace table and work things out." Master Gena sighed.

Gena saw the dragons fly over the village, heading toward the lake. Grabbing her parchment, she hurried to the beach.

When she got there, soldiers lined the perimeter, but this time they didn't let her through.

"Step aside this instance!" she demanded to a young soldier who blocked her path and avoided her eyes.

"Enough, Master Scholar. The soldier is doing his job." Lukas approached the line. "Let her through."

The soldier turned, and the scholar stormed past. "What is the meaning of this, Dragon *Master*?"

He let her tone go unremarked. "We must limit access to the dragon eggs."

"You mean the shells," she snapped.

"One and the same," he replied coolly.

She looked around. "Where are Ashton and Galileo?"

He shrugged. "They haven't been by."

"Will you let them in if they do?"

"No. They have no purpose here anymore. The dragons know what to do."

She looked at him sadly. "What is happening to you?"

Without a word, he guided her toward Rory. Gena approached the beast, making a wide path around the mother-to-be.

She bowed to him. He dipped his large head.

After that, there would be no more communication. Without Ashton around as a translator, Gena had little to do. She jotted down a description of the parent-to-be but couldn't even say if the dragon was male or female. Frustrated, she turned on Lukas.

"How am I supposed to go about my work without Ashton? She has been at the heart of this study from the beginning. She brought you on board."

"She didn't *bring* me; I followed her. She had no intention of sharing anything with me."

"Children!" Gena muttered under her breath as she left Lukas on the beach.

Chapter 41

"They are requiring us to plant that weed, but still taxing us at the rate our crops would have brought in. How is that fair?" a woman shouted.

Galileo raised his arms, trying to calm the twenty people gathered outside his cottage. Ashton stood by his side, fuming.

"They are selling the shells to other villages while our crops suffer," an old farmer said.

These complaints had been going on for fifteen minutes or more. Ashton couldn't stand it any longer. "How do you know?"

"Lieutenant Raquel reached out. The soldiers want my sister-in-law to drive the wagon; she refused," Frankel said, stepping forward.

She was relieved to see a friendly face.

"Who's leading this group of traders?" Ashton asked.

"Lukas. They're calling him Master of the Dragons."

Ashton's heart stopped. "Lukas? I can't believe he's betraying the people. I get that he's mad at me, but I didn't think he would stoop to this."

Her mind raced to look at all the options while the villagers stared at her expectantly.

"I heard the chancellor has ordered the production of dragon-killing mechanisms from the blacksmith," a young woman in front said.

Fear for the dragons ripped through Ashton, pushing past her anger at Brindisi. "And what side does the blacksmith lean toward?"

"It's simply a sale for her. She sees no reason not to fill it."

Now Nikolai had gone too far. Not only was he robbing Olmerta, but he also planned to cull the dragons as they did in the old days. That's what drove the dragons off to begin with. Ashton had a feeling Brindisi wasn't going to run away this time.

"Can you find out when the blacksmith must deliver the machines to the chancellor?"

The woman nodded.

"Let me know as soon as you do." She turned to Frankel. "Tell your sister-in-law to accept."

"What? Why? She doesn't want anything to do with the Cabots and their plans to ruin our farmers."

"It would give us an inside track. We'll know the movement of the shipment."

Murmurs throughout the crowd got her attention. She raised her voice to be heard. "It's hard to keep a secret with a group this large, but I'm counting on your help."

"You're only a girl. What can you do?"

Heat rose to her cheeks, and she swallowed the lump in her throat. "It's not about me. It's about saving the dragons and helping Olmerta prosper. Not to mention, keeping the villagers safe."

"Down with the Cabots!" rang out a male voice.

"We're with you!" someone shouted.

She forced a smile. "We'll take only what Olmerta has a right to. What should have been ours to begin with—no more. And we'll have no bloodshed. The people guarding the caravan are our neighbors."

"What if they don't give it up willingly?" Frankel asked.

"I'll think of something. For now, go about your work. Plant the dragon fire. The dragons need it, so we need it."

Slowly, the crowd broke up. The mood ran from doubtful to hopeful, but at least they didn't seem angry anymore. Frankel stayed behind with Galileo and Ashton.

She hugged him. "I'm so glad to see you. You look heathy."

"I tell Tomas he needs to stop feeding me so much or the dragons will pick me up next time for a snack." He smiled.

"What are you scheming, granddaughter?" Galileo asked.

"I only have the beginnings of a plan. I'm familiar with the route of the caravan and how they position their guards. What I can't be sure of is their reaction."

"We need to lure them away from the caravan," Frankel said. "Leave us fewer soldiers to deal with."

"Good idea. Now what about the blacksmith?" Ashton asked.

"Let me deal with her. I speak a language she can understand," Galileo said.

Ashton gave him a quizzical look but didn't probe further.

Chapter 42

From high in the tree and hidden from view, Ashton watched the wagons approach. When they reached the bend in the road, she released the chittering call of an oriole.

Moments later, the woods erupted with a loud bang and multiple screams.

"You three, go check that out," Lukas called to his soldiers. To the others, he said, "Keep the wagons moving."

The jittery horses lunged forward, anxious to escape the noise from behind.

When the tail of the small caravan rounded the bend, Ashton climbed down the tree in time to drop in front of the lead wagon. Fifteen others poured from the surrounding woods in front, with another twenty to the rear.

Lukas and the remaining two guards drew their swords.

"That won't be necessary," Ashton said from behind her mask. She spoke in a husky tone to disguise her identity, but she didn't think it would fool Lukas.

She was counting more on the arrows notched and aimed at their chests to convince them to give up easily.

"What are you after?" Lukas asked.

"Only what is rightly Olmerta's," she answered. "Drop your weapons."

The soldiers complied.

This was a little too easy, and Ashton was uncomfortable. She expected a trap to spring. Her eyes darted around the woods and down the trail, but she saw nothing amiss.

She signaled and men began pulling off tarps to reveal the contents of the wagons. "Here," one said.

Others joined him as he climbed into the wagon and placed eggshells into waiting canvas bags. When the bags were full, the runners faded into the trees. The man jumped down, and Ashton motioned for the villagers to retreat.

Without another word, she turned and ran for the village, anticipating the twang of bowstring and zip of an arrow to follow her. She didn't stop running until she was safely out of range, then she followed a circuitous route to the agreed-upon rendezvous point with her counterparts.

"They are changing the route this time," Frankel reported to Ashton days later as she dusted the shelves in the shop. "I'd be surprised if they didn't add more guards."

"Then we'll have to add more villagers. And it would be safer if we had a second ring waiting in case they have some people in reserve to trap us." She continued her cleaning as if planning to rob a caravan was just another task on her to-do list.

"Do you think they'll give up so easily a second time?"

She faced him. "Lukas isn't stupid. He isn't going to risk the lives of his soldiers over something as minor as eggshells. We didn't take anything extra, which I believe will buy us some goodwill. But we can't get sloppy. I don't want anyone on the front lines who may accidentally let loose an arrow and start the fighting."

"They won't fall for a distraction this time," Frankel said.

"Agreed. Do you have another suggestion?"

"What if we spook the horses? Get them to run and stretch out the procession?"

She thought about it. "It would cause a momentary stir of confusion, but the soldiers will recover quickly. Will your sister-in-law tell us in advance which wagon the eggshells will be in? That will help us get in and out quicker."

"I'll get her to mark it somehow." Frankel walked around the shop, running his fingers over some of the figurines. "It was a genius plan to slip every farmer a bit of the eggshell fertilizer without them knowing."

"That was Grandfather's idea. It gives them deniability with the benefit of added produce," Ashton said.

"Plus, with every farm yielding more, it'll be hard to prove the increase is because of the eggshells and not merely the growing season. You're messing up Master Gena's studies."

"She'll understand."

"We can't keep stealing the eggshells. We need a more sustainable logistics plan."

"I'm hoping the chancellor will get frustrated and give up. After all, he'll be able to collect more taxes from the increase in crops. Maybe that will satisfy him."

Frankel gave her a look that showed what he thought of that logic.

"Maybe we should let the next caravan go through. They'll think it was a one and done for us, and they'll drop their guard," she suggested.

"I like that. Let's send a few people out for reconnaissance though. See if they change their tactics."

Three weeks later, Ashton impatiently waited for the raiders to rendezvous after the second offensive.

As planned, they let the last caravan go through without making any moves. They only observed from a distance to see how the soldiers adjusted after the last attack.

Ashton learned a lot from the watchers of the caravan and had devised new plans, so when the raiders finally arrived, she was upset to see two people carrying a third person between them.

"What happened? Are you okay?"

"I'm fine. I tripped over a tree root. I wasn't even being chased."

Ashton's heart pounded loudly. The thought of someone getting hurt on her watch was not something she was prepared for. She leaned against a nearby tree and lowered herself to the ground.

Frankel sat beside her. "He's fine. A cold compress and he'll be good as new."

She hung her head. "What am I doing? This is dangerous."

"I have to give it to you; you know your tactics. We were ready for the second ring of soldiers and shut them down quickly. Lukas looked so cocky as he waited for them to come to his rescue." Frankel laughed.

Ashton attempted to smile, but it fell short. "We need a new plan."

Chapter 43

The roar shook the cottage, and Ashton jumped from her bed. She didn't bother with shoes as she ran toward the dragon's cry. Reaching out with her mind, she touched Rory and flinched at the hatred boiling from him.

"Rory, what is it?"

Another cry split the night, and Ashton passed others outside also searching for the cause. She continued her race to the beach.

As she broke through the bushes, she saw the steely-blue dragon draped over the body of a smaller purple beast.

"Rory, is she okay? Is she hurt?"

He swung his head toward her, smoke escaping his nostrils.

"Only humans could have done this. Tell me who it was," he demanded.

Ashton cautiously approached the hole in the sand. She blanched when she took in the tiny bodies of baby dragons, a pale, sickly color and not moving.

Then she cursed because of what she didn't see—eggshells.

"Who?" Rory's voice rang in her head again, so forcefully, Ashton was feeling ill.

"I don't know," she managed. "I don't know, but I'll find out. I promise you."

Galileo came stumbling from the path. Taking one look at the situation, tears came unbidden to his eyes. Ashton grabbed his arms. "Stay here with Rory. Don't let anyone else get near them. I don't know what might happen. At this point, they can't tell friend from foe."

"Where are you going?"

"I have to find Lukas. This is unimaginable. I can't believe he sank this low."

"Why do you think this was him?"

She motioned around the beach. "What's missing from this picture?"

Galileo looked at her blankly.

"Lukas has posted soldiers here around the clock from the time the eggs are laid until the shells are carted off. Why didn't they see the attack on the eggs? Why didn't they do anything?" She was so angry she was shaking.

"I need to find Lukas and figure out how we are going to mend fences with the dragons. Grandfather, did I cause this? Were my attacks on the wagons what forced Lukas to act before the dragonettes were even born?" Now she was crying too.

He held her, rocking gently as he rubbed her back. "Shhh, no, my sweet child. You didn't cause this atrocity. Only one greedy person is responsible, and I'm not talking about Lukas."

Another hand reached out to stroke Ashton's hair. She turned to face the master scholar who had joined them in their grief.

Gena's strong voice was strained as she said, "Some people have no thought beyond their evil desires. I wish I could say they didn't know any better, but it isn't true. This was done out of malice, not ignorance."

"I need to talk to Lukas. I need to know why this happened." Ashton hugged her grandfather, then sent a message to Rory that she would return soon.

In response, he shot a searing flame into the pit to consume the remains of the babies. Then he helped the parent-that-should-have-been launch into the sky.

Ashton ran through the trees as fast as her legs would carry her, not stopping for breath until she was standing on shaky legs in front of the gate to Lukas's house. Pacing back and forth a few times to get her breathing and her emotions under control, she pushed through the gate and marched to the front door.

The door flung open before Ashton had a chance to knock. "What was the awful sound?" Lukas's mother asked.

"Someone has attacked the dragon eggs," Ashton said.

"Another caravan? At this time of the night?"

"Not the wagons. The eggs in the sand before the dragons even hatched."

Melea covered her mouth with a trembling hand. "Come in, come in. What a shock." She looked Ashton over. "You don't even have shoes on."

In contrast, Melea was fully dressed, and a fire glowed in the hearth. "Why are you up so late? Besides the sound of the dragons, that is?" Ashton asked.

"My dear, you haven't heard? Lukas has been arrested. His father is at the palace now trying to get his brother to listen to reason."

Ashton's anger at Lukas turned to fear. Then she felt ashamed for even considering he could have been involved in something so horrible. "When did this happen?"

"After the second raid on the caravan. Nikolai claims Lukas played some part in the attacks." Melea looked closely at Ashton's face. "He didn't, did he?"

"No. No, of course not." Ashton shook her head furiously and wrapped her arms around Melea. Lukas's mother broke into tears. She must have been holding it together, not knowing whether her son would uphold his commitment to the palace or side with the villagers. Ashton wondered which one Melea found more comforting.

"What can I do?" Ashton asked.

Melea pulled away and wiped her eyes. "Nothing. Stephan is doing what he can. If he can't get through to his brother, no one will." She sank into a hardback chair.

Ashton kneeled beside her. "Could Nikolai have anything to do with the attack on the baby dragons?"

Squeezing her eyes closed, Melea nodded subtly. "He's obsessed. All he talks about are those shells and what he can do with the money he's going to collect from selling them. After the first shipment was stolen, I thought Nikolai was going to have a breakdown."

Guilt washed over her anew. Ashton had pushed Nikolai too far and made things worse. She was only trying to help.

"Ask Lukas to come see me when he gets home. I'm sure your husband will be successful in his release."

"Certainly." Melea took Ashton's hands in her own. "You've always been so close. I'm sure he could use a friend to lean on right now."

Biting her tongue to keep from confessing their fight to an already grieving mother, Ashton squeezed her hands, then withdrew.

Her trip through the woods was much longer as she walked, feeling every cut and bruise on the soles of her feet. When she reached the beach, Galileo and Gena were still together, fending off the curious, encouraging them to return home. Ashton broke the news about Lukas's arrest.

"There's your answer about why the soldiers weren't here," Galileo said.

"If Lukas were in charge, this never would have happened," Gena said.

Ashton wanted to scream. So much was happening, and she didn't know what to do.

Rory's return wasn't like his usual arrival on a warm breeze. It felt more like a gale-force wind, bringing moisture picked up from the lake.

Ashton approached him, speaking aloud for Gena and Galileo to hear. "I don't have an answer yet. Lukas has been arrested, and he's the one who leads the soldiers who usually guard the eggs."

"It was probably that scum chancellor," Galileo spat.

Gena put a calming hand on Galileo's arm. "We aren't sure of anything yet."

Ashton forced herself to stay calm and pass those feelings onto Rory. "We'll keep looking until we figure it out. I promise."

Rory rose up to his full height, causing her to crane her neck to look at him. She still felt his boiling anger, but also his attempt to control it.

"Brindisi is very unhappy. She's not interested in further dealings with the humans."

"But you need the sand for your eggs. Where will you go?"

"This beach is now ours," Rory said.

Chapter 44

Ashton hurried home to clean up and dress before heading to the palace. She needed to figure out how to get to Lukas and discover what was going on.

Gena stood before the front gates.

"What are you doing here?" Ashton asked.

"You can't go in alone. Do you have a plan?"

Ashton hesitated. "No, not really. But they have to let me see him."

"The chancellor doesn't *have* to do anything," Gena said in a tone Ashton remembered hearing from her mother.

She clenched her fists. "I can't stand by and do nothing."

The master scholar took her by the arm and walked her away from the palace. Once out of sight of the palace guards, Gena directed their stroll casually around the palace toward the barracks.

The usually orderly practice yard was abuzz with more soldiers mulling around than Ashton had ever seen in one place. They huddled in groups and talked in serious tones. There was none of the banter and bravado typically associated with these men and women.

"Ah, Lieutenant Raquel, just the person we were looking for," Master Gena said in her most authoritarian voice.

"Master Scholar, what a pleasure to see you, as always," Raquel replied formally but without a hint of a smile.

"I understand you have received some bad news," Gena said.

Raquel looked from Gena to Ashton. "I'm sure it's nothing more than a misunderstanding."

"Help us understand." The scholar led the way toward the barrack offices, not even checking to see if Raquel was following. She was.

When the three women got behind closed doors, Gena's demeanor relaxed visibly. "Tell us everything."

Raquel looked as if the weight of a dragon had been lifted from her shoulders. "Master Gena, they took Lukas yesterday right before shift change."

"Who took him?"

"The chancellor's personal guards. Lukas was giving out assignments, and they came into our barracks and hauled him away like a criminal. He told me to take over for him." Raquel threw her hands up in frustration.

"I tried, but they left one of their guards here. He said the chancellor put him in charge. He wouldn't let the next shift go to the beach, and he sent one of the personal guards to bring the rest to the barracks."

Gena nodded, encouraging her to go on.

"I asked to see the papers calling for his arrest, but the guard refused to show me. I think it has something to do with caravan heists." At this, Raquel shot a look at Ashton.

"I immediately went to Sir Stephan. He said he was going to talk to the chancellor. We're still waiting to hear any news," Raquel said.

248

"Do you know where they're holding him?" Ashton asked.

"Not for sure."

"Can you find out?"

"I'll do what I can."

"Let us know if you hear anything from Sir Stephan. I'll be in my cottage," Master Gena said. She opened the door, then turned to Raquel. "On second thought, meet us in my workshop directly after the second moon rises."

Raquel bowed and stayed behind as Ashton and Gena left the practice yard.

"Now what?" Ashton asked.

"I don't imagine Nikolai would put his nephew and heir to the throne in the dungeon. I suspect he only wanted Lukas out of the way for a time. But that's time we don't have if we're going to help the dragons."

"Will Sir Stephan be able to talk Nikolai into releasing Lukas?"

"Eventually. But not until after the damage is done. For now, go to work. Meet us tonight and we'll discuss options."

"Is it ready?" Nikolai barked without preamble.

The blacksmith bowed. "Yes, Chancellor. I built it to your exact specifications."

"Where is it? I want to see it work."

"I have it in the wagon out front."

Nikolai jumped from his seat. "Let's go at once."

He bounded down the front steps like a boy on his birthday as Bayard followed closely at his heels.

A large wagon hitched to two plow horses waited in front of the gates. The blacksmith released the tarp, then pulled it off with a flourish to reveal an oversized crossbow mounted on a five-foot tower. She climbed onto the wagon and pulled a safety pin from the base.

"It swivels so you can adjust aim as necessary." She then turned a knob on top, and the bow pivoted up and down.

Nikolai had to stop himself from pushing her aside to inspect his new toy. Instead, he forced himself to put on an air of skepticism. "Demonstrate that it works."

A crowd gathered to see what brought the chancellor out of his palace. They murmured as they watched, speculating as to the purpose of such a weapon.

The blacksmith dutifully loaded a bolt from a specially made quiver designed to hold the large projectiles. A series of pulleys took on much of the work to retract the oversized bowstring. She repositioned the crossbow to fire into the woods with a high arc. "Would you like to fire it?" she asked the chancellor.

This time, he couldn't stop himself from climbing into the wagon. The blacksmith pointed at the trigger, and Nikolai obliged. With a *thunk*, the wire released, and the bolt disappeared into the trees. It was a satisfying sound.

"Show me how to load it," Nikolai demanded.

The blacksmith walked him through the steps, and Nikolai adjusted the intended trajectory of the bolt. The crowd hurried out of the way as he swung around. Nikolai laughed in delight.

"Those oversized reptiles won't threaten Olmerta again!" he announced loud enough for all to hear. Then he pulled the trigger, sending a bolt flying over the palace.

As he swung his new toy around again to aim into the crowd, he took joy in watching the townspeople run away in fear.

Chapter 45

Late the next day, Ashton still hadn't heard anything about Lukas's release, and she was worried. She finished closing the store while Galileo puttered in the workshop on new designs that included dragon eggs.

The bell to the door jingled. A frenzied Frankel rushed to the counter. "Ashton, you have to come to the beach."

"What's wrong?" she asked.

"The dragons are gathering."

Galileo came from the workroom, wiping his hands on a rag. "What do you mean gathering?"

"I mean a lot of them. I know dragons always look frightening, but this time, I swear they're pissed."

Ashton took off her working apron and tossed it on the counter. "Frankel, find as many of the dragon talkers as you can. Have them meet us at the beach. Grandfather, see how many more haven't been tested yet. This isn't the ideal time, but we must get through to as many dragons as possible. I'll go to the beach and try to talk Rory down."

She reached out to Rory and told him she was on her way. He grunted an acknowledgment.

She started the conversation before she set eyes on him. "Why are you all here? What do you need?"

"Your soldiers cannot protect us. We'll fend for ourselves."

A shiver ran down her spine. This was escalating out of control.

"I understand you need to protect yourselves. I don't blame you. Is there to be another clutch?"

"Yes, and there will be no issues with this one."

"Of course. I understand." She broke through the trees and stopped in her tracks at the sight of twenty or more dragons on the beach, creating a wall between the forest and the water. Between their wings, Ashton recognized the ebony black she had seen on no other dragon than Brindisi.

Ashton reached out to the queen. "I know you're angry. What can I do to help?"

"There is nothing you can do. Your word to protect the eggs cannot even be trusted."

That stung, but she was right.

Frankel hurried to Ashton's side. "I found a few. They're scared but they want to help."

"They can probably feel the anger coming from the dragons."

"I can feel the anger, and I don't have any connection!"

Frankel led Ashton to where the handful of villagers huddled nervously. This was very different from their first encounter with the beasts.

"It'll be okay. They aren't angry at you. Someone killed dragon eggs, and they want to make sure it doesn't happen again. So do we," Ashton explained.

"What do you what us to do?" a man barely out of his teens asked.

"See if you can reach any of the dragons. Remind them we are on their side. Try to pass on feelings of calm."

"And how are we supposed to do that? I'm scared half to death," an old man said.

"I know it isn't easy, but just as you can feel their anger, if you project a sense of calmness, they can feel it. We don't want this to get worse."

"Try singing," Frankel suggested.

They all turned to stare at him at once.

"Doesn't singing calm you when you're scared? Does it calm your small children? It does mine."

Ashton nodded decisively. "Great idea. Sing to them."

"What should we sing?" someone asked.

Trying not to let her frustration show, she blurted out the first song she could think of. "*Look to the East.*"

Immediately the group began to chatter, refreshing their memories with the words.

Ashton approached Rory again. "Why is Brindisi here?"

"It is her time."

"Time for what?"

Rory cocked his head. "Why else would we come to this sand?"

"She's having a clutch!" Ashton was so surprised, she blurted it out loud.

"Of course."

"I thought she was too old."

"While it is unusual for a queen to lay a clutch, it is very significant. It means the next queen is coming," Rory said.

"The next queen?"

"We live a long time in human years, but not forever. Just as the previous Brindisi hatched this queen, so shall this queen bring forth the next one."

While Ashton pondered this, the words the villagers were singing seeped into her head.

"*Safe beneath their watchful eyes . . .*"

The dragons didn't relax their vigilance, but they did seem to be calmer. Even Brindisi's burning rage wasn't quite as hot.

Sand flew from the pit the dragons were digging to prepare for the queen's clutch. They were much more efficient than the shovels Ashton and Galileo had used.

Although Ashton could barely see through the throng of dragons, Brindisi's black shape moved like a shadow behind her protectors. Ashton reached out to her through the *sentsentia*, but the queen was closed to her.

"This is not a time to talk to her. She has not had a successful clutch in many years," Rory said. "This may be her last chance. We will not allow anything to interfere."

"What can I do?"

"The music was a good idea."

Ashton smiled. "That was Frankel. He's a father, so he gets it."

They listened for a while.

"How long will you stay here?" she asked.

"Until the hatching."

"Even Brindisi?"

"Especially the queen. She will not leave their safety to chance."

Galileo advanced warily. When Ashton noticed him, she spoke so he could hear. "Brindisi is clutching."

He started, then recovered. "That's wonderful! Is that what all this excitement is about?"

"Mostly." She looked past him. "Did you find anyone who wants to connect with the dragons?"

"A few. They're with the others." He gestured toward the singers.

"Rory, we want to do whatever we can to repair the damage between humans and dragons," Ashton said. "Can we try to find others who are dragon talkers?"

"After the clutch is safely buried."

"Grandfather, the dragons are going to be here until the hatching, so we have time."

"I know what we need!" he said and hurried off.

Ashton looked quizzically after him and saw Gena among the singers. She had her parchment out and was scribbling furiously. When Ashton looked over her shoulder, she noted lines and arrows connecting many names.

"What's all this?"

Gena finished her sketch. "It's amazing really. Do you know most of these people are related to you?"

Ashton looked at the group, now in their fourth or fifth song. "Sure, some of them are distant cousins, but it's a small town. Of course there's going to be some relations."

Gena shook her head. "No, *all* the known dragon talkers are related to you somehow on your mother's side, even if it goes back more than three generations. A few of those Galileo brought to be tested are also related to you. If my suspicion is correct, only they will be able to speak to the dragons."

"Why? What is it about us?"

"I have no idea. That will be the next step."

"What about my grandparents? They are both dragon talkers."

"I have a feeling the charts will show a very distant cousin relationship between them," Gena said.

The dragons shifted about, drawing Ashton's attention. Then they trumpeted for all to hear. The sound was deafening. Many in the singing group covered their ears.

Once again, sand flew as the eggs were covered.

"There is a black egg," Rory said.

Chapter 46

"Is that good?" Ashton asked.

"Very good. The new queen is almost here," Rory said.

Galileo burst through the trees onto the sand. "What's happened now?"

"We're getting a new queen." Ashton smiled.

"A new queen?" Gena joined them. "What happens to this one?"

Ashton's face dropped. "Is Brindisi going to be okay?" she asked Rory.

"It is the natural order of things. She still has time. She must raise this young queen to be prepared to lead."

After relaying this to the others, Ashton asked her grandfather, "Where did you run off to?"

"I thought our guests might be hungry." At that moment, a herd of cattle broke through the trees, being prodded along by farmers. At the sight of the dragons, the cows in the front dug their hoofs into the sand, but they were pushed forward by the ones following.

"For your wing," Ashton told Rory.

He must have relayed the message, for one by one, the dragons stepped forward to claim a snack,

258

but only after the largest two were deposited in front of Brindisi.

Ashton hugged her grandfather. "Great thinking."

"I know from Rosa and your mother how much work giving birth is. If they are going to stand guard for days, the others will need their strength."

"Can we test the dragon talkers now?" Gena asked.

When Rory approved, Gena brought the untested villagers forward. The look of delight and amazement on their faces made it obvious when a connection was established.

At Gena's excitement, it was equally obvious that her assumption was correct. She made a few last notes, then looked up. "All relatives! I need to do some more research to trace your family history," she told Ashton. With that, she was off.

Ashton shook her head in awe of the master scholar's energy.

"Our thanks to Rosa's mate," Rory said. "A queen hatching should not take as long. She has been receiving the bulk portion of the red plant under the mountain."

"That's great news," she replied. Inwardly, and hidden from Rory, she was relieved the dragons wouldn't be near Silent Lake for long. She wasn't sure how Nikolai would react, but she was pretty sure it wouldn't be good.

"Perfect! This is outstanding!" Nikolai clapped his hands together. "What a wonderful opportunity to demonstrate my new toy!"

"They've been there all night," Bayard said. "And don't show any signs of leaving."

"Send birds with a message for the mayors of Melak, Daegu, and Busan to come at once. They need to see the slaughter firsthand. Requests for more machines will come from all over. We may need another forge to keep up with the demand."

"As you wish," Bayard said.

"But first, let's go have a chat with my nephew and share this fabulous news."

At the approach of the chancellor, the two guards at the door came to attention.

"Unlock it," Nikolai ordered.

One guard hurried to obey, fumbling with the key in his haste.

When the chancellor entered the room, Lukas automatically came to attention, but Nikolai saw the hatred in his eyes. That made this news even sweeter.

"It seems your beastly buddies are having a picnic on my beach."

Lukas kept quiet.

"I thought I'd visit them tomorrow. You see, I have a special treat for them. Something that will make me far more money than dragon eggs and with a more immediate return."

The boy's brooding was almost as irritating as his father's begging.

"You should want to be on the winning side of this encounter. This is the future of Olmerta. Not that I think you'll be heir much longer. I have been busy, after all."

"I never asked to be heir," Lukas spat.

"Ah, he does speak. I thought perhaps my guards cut out your tongue when they caught you conspiring against me." Nikolai strolled to a chair by the hearth and made himself comfortable.

"I didn't ask for you either, but I've been so busy ruling, I haven't put much effort into producing an offspring I can mold into a true Cabot leader. Your father is weak, but I thought I saw a spark in you. Apparently I was wrong."

He inspected his hands and freshly polished nails. "I've changed my priorities now. Soon you'll be replaced."

"No need to keep me locked up here then," Lukas said.

"I wouldn't want you to get hurt. Things are heating up out there. Haven't you heard? Oh, I guess not. News doesn't travel very quickly through a locked door."

"What's going on?"

"Those overgrown pests have outlived their welcome. But they have finally answered my call. The herd has descended—"

"It's a wing."

Startled by the interruption, Nikolai looked at his nephew. "What's a wing?"

"A group of dragons. We have families and villages; they have wings."

Nikolai chuckled. "Of course they do. And how did you come by this information?"

When Lukas didn't answer, Nikolai went on. "Your sympathies are starting to show, boy. Are you ready to tell me who was behind the eggshell stealing?"

"Are you ready to tell me who attacked my caravan and killed my soldiers?"

Their eyes met, neither willing to be the first to look away.

Chapter 47

It had been a long, uneventful night on the beach. Brindisi finally allowed Ashton to talk with her.

"Do queens always lay black eggs?" Ashton asked.

"Only one is black. That is the designated queen."

"What if she doesn't want to be queen?"

She felt Brindisi's derision. "Why would she not want to lead her wing?"

Ashton thought about Lukas. "Not everyone wants to rule."

"It is a duty and honor to serve in this way."

"What if she isn't a good leader?"

"She will have the support of the whole wing. They are the ones who make her a good queen," Brindisi said.

Ashton heard them before she saw them. Palace guards stomped through the forest, storming onto the sliver of sand the dragons hadn't occupied. Some were on horseback, although the horses were none too happy about being close to the giant beasts. The guards looked pretty frightened themselves when they took in the creatures they were up against.

Jumping to her feet, Ashton ran to the villagers who were still gathered nearby, talking with their new dragon friends.

"Stay back. Don't get caught in the middle if the dragons turn on the guards."

"What is the meaning of this?" Brindisi roared into Ashton's head.

"I don't know, but it isn't good. These are the chancellor's men, not Lukas's."

The dragons were on instant alert, the dragon talkers forgotten.

"Now what do we do?" a man asked Ashton.

"Stay out of the way," she said.

"This is our chance," she heard Gena hiss in her ear.

In all the excitement, she hadn't noticed the master scholar. "Come with me."

Together, they worked their way around the guards and faded into the trees. In the center of town, handpicked villagers had gathered and were awaiting the next phase of the plan.

"With so many of the guards away from the palace, this is the perfect time to get to Lukas," Gena said.

"Does Raquel know?"

"I sent her a message before I came to get you. Watch for her." Gena left Ashton to give instructions to the villagers.

When Ashton spotted Raquel in the shadows beside the palace, she hurried to her, resisting the urge to run.

"Lukas is in the east wing, third floor. Most of the palace guards are gone, so there's no one at his door." Raquel slipped Ashton a key. "Lock the door behind you and leave the key behind the large wall sconce in the hallway. I'll return it."

"Where will you be?"

"In front of the chancellor. He's called for me. I have a feeling he wants the soldiers as a shield against the dragons."

Ashton gripped Raquel's arm. "Thank you for this."

"Lukas is my commander." With that, Raquel walked slowly toward her appointment with Nikolai.

Ashton joined Gena and flashed her the key. "Let's move."

The villagers left for their assignments. Gena and Ashton entered the front door of the palace past the two guards still on duty there. Once inside, the halls were empty except for a servant scurrying through occasionally. Gena led them with purpose to the staircase, without glancing around.

"Stop fidgeting, child. You're going to give us away. No one will question the master scholar on a mission."

Ashton stuffed her hands inside her tunic to stop the shaking. She held her head up and tried not to think of the battle about to take place on the sands of Silent Lake.

As promised, no one guarded Lukas's door. While Gena watched the hall, Ashton fitted the key to the lock. When she pushed open the door, Lukas was pacing the floor. When he saw her, his eyes flew open wide, and he froze in his tracks.

The next moment, he had his arms around her, and she took in his woodsy scent as she hugged him.

"Enough of that already," Gena said. "We have work to do."

Lukas dropped his arms but took Ashton's hand. "We have to get to Rory. Uncle Nikolai is planning something terrible."

"How do you know?" she asked.

"Nikolai was in here gloating yesterday. He said he's going to show the dragons he's in charge. If they want access to the beach, they have to play by his rules."

"Lukas, the dragons have gathered at the beach right now!"

"Quickly, we need to stop Nikolai!" He rushed out of the room with the women closely following.

Ashton stopped to lock the door and hide the key. Gena held Lukas in place at the end of the hall until a loud ruckus came from the front entry.

Four palace guards rushed past them without turning their heads. Then Gena marched out first, signaling when it was clear. The rear entrance was left unguarded, and the trio slipped into the courtyard, making their way to the barracks unseen.

Chapter 48

Ashton's head pounded with the emotions emanating from the dragons on the beach. The closer she got, the stronger the connection. Lukas put his arm around her waist, helping her along.

"Can you block them out?" he asked.

"I'm trying, but there are so many. And they are beyond angry."

On the beach, black scorch marks dotted the area near the trees where palace guards previously stood.

Gena led them to the huddled dragon talkers. Galileo took Ashton into his arms. "What did we miss?" she asked.

An old man spoke up. "Those stupid guards don't know when to leave well enough alone. Even after the dragons fried the first one, they tried again." He pointed to the still-smoldering bodies. "They got eight before the others hightailed it out of here."

"The dragons can take care of themselves," Gena said.

"Not against the machine Nikolai was raving about outside my cell door. It was made specifically to hunt dragons," Lukas said.

As if on cue, a large wagon pulled by two plow horses wheeled to the edge of the trees and stopped. Nikolai and three other men sat on their horses under the cover of the trees. Raquel and a squad of soldiers marched forward, placing themselves between the dragons and the wagon.

"No!" Lukas cried, running to them. Ashton followed, stumbling along the way.

"Rory, it's Lukas," Ashton screamed inside her head. "Don't hurt him!"

Lukas got in Raquel's face. "What are you doing here?"

"My job, sir." But the conviction was not in her words.

Lukas turned to his uncle. "What are you thinking? Look at what the dragons did to your palace guards. Why are you putting my soldiers at risk?"

If Nikolai was surprised to see Lukas, he didn't react. "Your soldiers? I thought I paid their salaries."

"The people of Olmerta pay their salaries. You skim off the top," Lukas said.

The blacksmith was busy on the wagon, adjusting one knob, then another.

"Stop this, uncle. We can live in peace with the dragons."

Nikolai turned to the three mayors. "Does this look like peace to you? My guards are dead—roasted by dragon fire. They could turn on us at any time. We can't stand for this."

The three on horseback shrank farther into the trees.

Nikolai didn't notice or didn't care. "I have a way to clear our shores of these pests. But once they leave us, they might descend on your town. It's best to get ahead of it. My blacksmith will have another one ready by the end of the week."

This time, the mayors clamored to be heard over their neighbors, all placing bids on the dragon killing machine they were promised.

Meanwhile, Ashton appealed to Brindisi. "These soldiers mean you no harm. Nikolai is only using them as shields. Please don't hurt them."

"Your humans support this leader."

"No, I told you they don't. Look at the villagers who are here supporting you. Others brought you food. It's this one man stirring up trouble."

Suddenly, the ground began to shake. Lukas caught Ashton before she fell. Brindisi's frantic thoughts filled her head.

The queen was digging furiously at the sand, uncovering her eggs, all thought of the chancellor and his threat brushed aside.

Caught up in Brindisi's emotions, Ashton rushed to her side, wanting to help in the digging but knowing it was ridiculous. The other dragons kept their focus on the machine and the soldiers.

Three of the eggs had already hatched, and the dragonettes were fighting their way out of the sand. Brindisi scooped them from the hole and set them on level ground. Immediately, they began their waddle toward the water.

A shout directed Ashton's attention toward the woods closest to the lake. While all attention had been on the war machine, palace guards had crept around the center and were setting up firing positions from behind the rocks.

The dragon talkers ran to the water's edge, lining up to create a corridor for the dragonettes to safely pass through. Using the dropped armor from dead palace guards, sleeping mats, and random pieces of driftwood for protection, they warded off most of the arrows shot from the rocks. Their presence at least blocked the view, making it harder for the guards to aim.

The dragons had formed a barricade around the queen, who was still waiting for the other eggs to hatch. The black egg rocked fiercely.

"Fire!" Nikolai yelled.

The blacksmith fumbled with a bolt, dropped it, and tried again.

"Idiot!" the chancellor bellowed. He jumped from his horse and climbed on the wagon, pushing aside the blacksmith.

Rory took to the sky, circling over the lake and coming back for a good angle at the rocks. His first pass set fire to the nearby trees, clearing his approach for the next path.

The chancellor loaded the bolt, pulled the pin, and swiveled the crossbow to aim at Rory.

"Look out!" Ashton called.

Rory spun and the bolt flew by.

Nikolai let out a stream of curses as he loaded another bolt.

The torrent of fire Rory released on the guards hiding in the rocks was inescapable. Ashton didn't feel the slightest sympathy as the men screamed.

This time, the bolt Nikolai fired hit Rory square in the chest. The dragon barely reacted as the projectile shattered on impact. He continued his path up and over the trees, aligning himself for the next pass.

Nikolai loaded another bolt and waited.

Ashton was torn between watching the fight and watching the efforts of the new queen as she tried to break free from her egg. The other two eggs had hatched, and now five dragonettes fed in the lake. Three dragons had joined them in the water, ensuring they didn't return to the sand and the chaos.

Rory's shadow covered Ashton briefly as he made directly for the crossbow.

"Down!" Raquel shouted.

Without hesitation, the soldiers hit the sand, protecting their heads with their shields.

Nikolai waited until Rory was practically on top of him before he fired. The shattered bolt pieces fell on the chancellor's head as Rory's talons dug into his flesh, pulling him from the wagon.

His scream sounded as the black egg finally broke in two. The dragonette seemed to call out in answer. Brindisi lifted the coal-black dragon from the pit, placing her on the beach where she stumbled and rolled, becoming coated in sand.

The dragon talkers still lined her path to the water, and they watched in fascination as this little one waddled past.

When Ashton thought to look, the men on horseback had all fled, the crossbow was alight, and the soldiers were cheering.

When the dragonettes had their fill, they took to the sky. One by one, the adult dragons followed them.

The beach suddenly felt very empty without the monstrous creatures. Ashton found Galileo and hugged him tightly. The excited dragon talkers gathered around her, all hugging and smiling. She looked for Lukas near his soldiers, but he was nowhere to be seen.

Chapter 49

After loading the cart and transporting the shells back to her cottage, Master Gena had sent Ashton home to rest.

Now they were back to work, shoulder to shoulder. They wanted to distribute the shells as quickly as possible. Ashton inspected of the eggshells, taking notes, sorting, and preparing the fertilizer as the master scholar directed. They marveled at the thickness and color of the black egg.

"Do the black shells have special properties? More special, I mean," Ashton said.

Gena took the piece Ashton handed her. "I'm not sure, but I would like to set them aside for now. From what Rory has told you, queens are not born often. We don't want to squander this opportunity to study the shells. You are adding this information to your leather book, aren't you?"

"I need to add more pages. I also want to include some of the pages Grandmother left in the mountain."

"I'll help you with the binding as soon as we finish with this. It's not something to be put off. That's how information is lost. People put things off until later, but later never comes." Gena packed away the black shards in a velvet-lined box and carried it into her sleeping quarters.

She found Ashton staring out the window on her return. "Do you think Lukas is all right?" Ashton asked.

"He's a strong boy. He'll be fine."

"But I haven't heard a word from him. It's been a whole day."

Gena put her arm around Ashton's shoulders, guiding her back to the table. "He's behind closed doors with his advisors. There is a succession plan to enact. I'm sure he'll be busy for days."

"What if his advisors pressure him to follow in Nikolai's footsteps?" She couldn't keep the worry out of her voice.

"Lukas's loyalties have always been to Olmerta." Gena handed Ashton a shell to measure and crush for the fertilizer.

"I feel guilty for doubting his intentions, even for a moment," the young lady admitted.

The master scholar put a hand on Ashton's arm. "He was angry and hurt. You both probably said things you shouldn't have."

Ashton sighed. "I wish I knew what he was feeling. Nikolai was his uncle, after all."

Gena sniffed. "There's no love lost there. His uncle had him arrested."

"Still, it can't be easy for him. Now he has so much on his shoulders."

"Lukas has his father to guide him. He'll be a fine leader.

"But he never wanted any of this. Can't Earl Stephan take up the mantle?"

"Lukas must do what's right for Olmerta. It's between him and his advisors." Gena scribbled notes on a parchment.

"Stop telling me what I *can't* do and tell me what I can!" Lukas pushed damp hair off his forehead and slumped in his chair.

"I think we need to take a break," Stephan said. "Leave us."

The older men and women in the council chambers pushed back their chairs and exited, still arguing amongst themselves.

"Surely Uncle Nikolai did not put up with this kind of banter." Lukas folded his arms on the table and laid down his head. "They give me such a headache!"

Stephan barely hid a smirk. "No, my brother would not have been as patient as you have been. I feel your advisors are taking advantage of the situation and are trying to enact changes they have been pushing for years."

"Why does it have to all come at once? It's too much." The wooden table muffled his voice.

"The pace will slow when the excitement wears down. No one was particularly fond of Nikolai."

"Except that simpering weasel Bayard. Where is he anyway?"

"Lieutenant Raquel took the liberty of locking him in the dungeon until you see fit to hear his offenses against Olmerta." Stephan shuffled the papers in front of him.

Lukas peered over his crossed arms. "What offenses exactly? Wasn't he just following orders?"

"I understand she's still coming up with the list, but I believe ignoring common courtesies and personal hygiene are on the top."

"That's not really a legal requirement, is it?"

He laughed. "No, but don't be surprised if she asks you to write it into the law." Then his countenance turned serious. "Anyway, following orders isn't an excuse for breaking the law."

"That reminds me." Lukas sat up and rang the bell next to his seat.

The door behind him opened and a young page scurried in.

Removing a leather thong from around his neck, he passed it to the boy. "Take this key straight away to Master Gena. Tell her she has full access to the vaults whenever she wishes. Can you remember that?"

The boy gave a slight bow with a fist over his chest.

Gently, Lukas moved the page's left arm down and replaced it with his right one. "There you go. Be off."

The boy bowed again and slipped away.

Galileo watched Ashton pack food into her saddlebags. "Do you have to go now?"

"There's nothing for me to do here. I'm going stir crazy waiting for Lukas to summon me. I've left him several messages at the palace and with his mother."

"He has a lot on his mind."

"I know, I know. But so do I. I want to see how Brindisi is doing with her young ones." She swung herself into the saddle. "I won't be gone long."

She nudged Sheba, and they started their trek to the foothills of the mountains.

Before she reached the dark woods, she recognized the familiar shapes in the sky. Rory swooped down close enough to blow Ashton's short hair around.

"Well met, Rory," Ashton said, using *sentsentia*. "How is your queen and her dragonettes?"

"They are in training already," he replied. "See how strong their wings are?"

Ashton took in the smaller dragons dipping and careening through the air playfully. As she watched, two collided and fell awkwardly for several minutes before righting themselves.

"And where is Brindisi?"

"I am here," came an unfamiliar voice in her head.

She started, giving Rory a strange look. "Was that you?"

Rory's expression almost looked exuberant. "So you hear the young Brindisi." It was a statement, not a question. "That is a good sign."

A shadow rushed at Ashton, stopping short of pushing her over before landing with a thud in front of Sheba. The horse tried to skitter away, but Ashton held her fast.

Stroking the mare's neck as she climbed from the saddle, Ashton spoke calming words. Then she turned her attention to the newcomer.

Bowing at the waist, Ashton addressed the shadow in *sentsentia*. "Welcome, young Brindisi. I trust you and your mother are well."

"Are you the Ashton Brindisi speaks of?"

"I am. And I was there at your birth."

"I heard you. Your voice is loud and clear." The dragonette tilted her head to the side. "You are still frightened of something."

"No danger to you or yours, I assure you. Only . . . human issues." *How do you explain such complicated human emotions to a newborn dragon?*

Rory must have been in on the conversation, for he spoke up. "Brindisi will be most interested to hear you have established a bond so easily and so early."

"Is that unusual?" Ashton asked.

"It's been many years since we have experienced it, but yes. Usually only a dragon of many cycles can reach a human," Rory explained.

The black dragonette was only a few days old but already stood taller than Ashton's head. She hopped and shuffled circles around Sheba and Ashton as if having trouble controlling her feet.

"Perhaps you need to spend more time on your land lessons and less on flying for the moment," Rory said to the young one.

With a snort and a puff of smoke, the shadow launched into the sky.

Ashton felt Rory's laughter in her chest. She stayed to watch as more dragonettes joined the dots in the sky.

"It's been many years since we have had this many young ones in our midst. The wing is hopeful again." Rory settled down on his haunches.

"What about the members of the wing who were causing trouble? The ones who took our soldiers?"

"They have been banned from the mountain for a time. Once they learn what is like to fend for themselves, they may return, and this time they will listen to the wisdom of Brindisi."

When Ashton finally turned toward home, she felt lighthearted. Seeing the fruits of her labor in the form of healthy dragonettes gave her the strength to approach Lukas once again with the hope he would listen to her pleas.

She had to convince him the wellbeing of the dragons was also good for Olmerta.

Chapter 50

Back at work in the master scholar's cottage, Ashton focused on her handwriting as she copied the instructions Gena had given her. They were to be distributed to the farmers when they picked up the fertilizer that morning. Gena wanted the farmers to keep meticulous notes on usage and results so she could perfect her mixture.

A commotion in the front yard drew her to the window. "Master Gena, come quickly."

Gena joined her at the window as they watched Lukas approach with his troops in formation behind him.

The master scholar moved to open the door.

Fear took hold of Ashton. She gripped Gena's arm. "Wait! He's chancellor now. What if he's here to confiscate the shells?"

"We won't know what he wants until we give him a chance, will we?" Gena stepped out the door, Ashton close on her heels.

A crowd had gathered, obviously curious to see the soldiers in dress uniforms. The farmers waiting for their fertilizer grew silent as the soldiers came to a stop in front of the women.

Ashton approached her closest friend, not sure of his intent, arriving with forces to back him up. "Lukas, please. Let us distribute the shells fairly using Master Gena's schedule. It will benefit all of Olmerta, you'll see," she said.

Lukas was so serious, it frightened her.

"You're the chancellor now. You can make things right. You don't have to be like your uncle," she went on.

Why isn't he saying anything? He's only staring.

Suddenly, he dropped to one knee. All the soldiers behind him did the same. As if on cue, Master Gena stepped forward, handing him a package. He unwrapped it and held it out to Ashton.

It was the golden crown with the royal blue sapphire that matched her eyes. Ashton was speechless. It was real, and it was beautiful.

Lukas finally spoke. "Anyone who knows you recognizes the queen in your blood. The master scholar has confirmed it through the archives to the satisfaction of the council. As you have led Olmerta through reuniting with the dragons, so shall you lead us into the future."

She was frozen. Surely this was a dream. They had been working all night. Maybe she had fallen asleep standing up.

"You have to take the crown," Lukas whispered.

Ashton only stared at him as if she were watching the action, not as a participant. She waited with anticipation to see what would happen next.

"Oh my goodness," Master Gena said. She took the crown and placed it on Ashton's head.

The others still standing dropped to one knee. "Long live Queen Ashton," someone cried. More people took up the chant.

Lukas's face broke into a large grin. "Can we get up now?"

"Get up, get up," she called, waving her arms. When Lukas stood in front of her, she buried her face in his chest, gripping him firmly. The crowd cheered again.

Chapter 51

"I don't think a queen needs to be cleaning shelves," Master Gena told Ashton when she entered the Silent Mountain Shop.

"As a queen, I can clean if I want to."

"Welcome, Master Scholar," Galileo greeted her from his stool behind the counter. "And what brings you here this beautiful afternoon?"

"You are certainly in a good mood."

"Business is booming. As you can see, I can barely keep the product on the shelf."

"All business in Olmerta should increase very soon. With the dragons safely laying eggs on the shores of Silent Lake again, we'll have plenty of shells to go around, which will boost crop productions, thereby getting more brakons to change hands."

"What wonderful news," Galileo said.

"We're also experimenting with the shells to see what else they may be good for. Perhaps they also have healing properties or could be good for the herd animals."

The bell chimed, and the blacksmith entered. Ashton stiffened.

The blacksmith set a wrapped package on the counter. "Galileo, while I appreciate your generosity,

I did what I did for free. You provided me the way out." She patted his hand and left the shop without another word.

Gena raised an eyebrow at Galileo.

He gingerly unwrapped the package, exposing the glossy, black obsidian of Brindisi—Galileo's prized possession.

"Grandfather, you gave Brindisi away?" Ashton was incredulous.

"I was trading this Brindisi for another one."

Gena started to laugh. "It wasn't a fluke that those bolts shattered, was it?"

"You sell our blacksmith short. She's more than capable of crafting a proper weapon. You heard her. She was in a bad situation with the chancellor and was looking for a way out. I helped her think of one." Galileo caressed the statue.

"Very wise, Galileo. I could use your help on the project I'm working on for the queen." Gena glanced at Ashton. "She just doesn't know it yet."

Ashton shook her head and smiled.

"Do you have time now?" Gena asked.

"For you, of course, Master Scholar." He stood and removed his apron. "Lead the way."

They passed Lukas entering as they left the shop.

"What's up with them?" he asked Ashton. "They look like they are up to something."

She laughed. "I haven't seen Grandfather this happy since before Grandmother left."

Lukas plopped down on a bench and watched Ashton work. "Don't you have other things you should be working on?"

She turned to face him. "I don't know how to be a queen."

"You need to be yourself."

"Brindisi said it's the wing who makes the queen."

"Then you're set. Keep looking out for the best interests of Olmerta like you have been," Lukas said.

"I'm so grateful your father agreed to be my right hand. I thought he'd be upset with me for how things turned out. Rightfully you're next in line."

"Are you kidding? I never wanted to be chancellor. Neither did my father. Allowing him to help right some of the wrongs of the Cabot name is more than he could ask for. Mother's also happy because Father's much more relaxed." Lukas leaned against the wall. "It is kind of strange that Nikolai never produced an heir of his own."

"Not that strange." Ashton's smile lit her face. "Master Gena was slipping something into his food to keep him sterile . . . and often impotent."

Lukas burst with laughter.

Ashton sat down next to him. "She said she couldn't allow his maliciousness to continue. Her hope was, with you as chancellor, things would turn for Olmerta."

"And now we have seated the rightful queen, thanks to Master Gena. Her research into your ancestry was enough to convince my advisors that you were in line for the throne. Trust me, they weren't fighting the idea of having you as a leader. They only needed documentation to back up their decision."

"She's so happy to be working in the vault. You couldn't have given her a better treasure. It's going to take her ages to research and catalog everything."

"She's training new scholars, so she'll have plenty of help," Lukas said.

"What's happening with the palace guards?"

"Raquel is interviewing each of them to determine the level of their involvement."

She nodded.

"I gave her a promotion based on her excellent judgment on the beach. She never had any intention of protecting Nikolai, even if it meant serious consequences for her later."

"She's a great soldier and leader. You're lucky to have her," Ashton said.

They sat in silence for a moment, lost in their thoughts.

"I can't believe Frankel's family turned down the offer to drive the wagons the first time. I practically gift-wrapped the caravan for you," Lukas said.

"You counted on people to be as devious as you are. Some have stronger morals than that."

His face fell. "You know I never changed course. I was always on your side."

"You could have been more clear. Why all the secrecy?"

"I didn't know who was spying for Nikolai. I couldn't take any chances. He knew we were friends."

"Were?" she asked.

He nudged her with his shoulder. "Were and are. Nothing will ever change that."

"Nothing?"

"Are you sending me to the dungeon or something?"

Ashton harrumphed. "You can be so annoying."

Lukas turned serious. Gently taking her chin in his hand, he leaned close, brushing her lips with his.

A shiver ran down her spine, and her heart quickened.

"*Best* friends," he whispered. "Forever."

From The Author

Fantasy is my favorite genre to read. Anne McCaffrey inspired me with her Dragonriders of Pern series. But because I always read fantasy, I struggled to create a fresh idea to write one.

For my birthday in 2019, my daughter Paige wrote me the poem *Silent Mountain* and a few opening scenes to stir my imagination. It was the best birthday present I've ever received.

I was finally able to put words on paper for what has become *The Dragons of Silent Mountain*.

About the Author

Dawn Brotherton is an award-winning author, Air Force veteran and avid quilter. Her variety of interests has led to a variety of genres including thriller, cozy mystery, romance, young adult fantasy, middle grade sports, picture books, and nonfiction.

Keep in touch with Dawn via the web:
Website:
https://www.dawnbrothertonauthor.com/
Facebook:
https://www.facebook.com/DawnBrothertonAuthor
Instagram:
https://www.instagram.com/dawnbrothertonauthor/
Bookbub:
https://www.bookbub.com/authors/dawn-brotherton

Other Books by Dawn Brotherton

Jackie Austin Mysteries
The Obsession (also available on audio)
Wind the Clock

Eastover Treasures

Romance
Untimely Love

Lady Tigers Series
Trish's Team (book 1)
Margie Makes a Difference (book 2)
Nicole's New Friend (book 3)
Avery Appreciates True Friendship (book 4,
written by Paige Ashley Brotherton)
Tammy Tries Baseball (book 5)

Picture Book
If I Look Like You
Scout and Her Friends Activity Book

Nonfiction
Baseball/Softball Scorebook
The Road to Publishing

Contributing Author to
A-10s Over Kosovo
Water from Wellspring